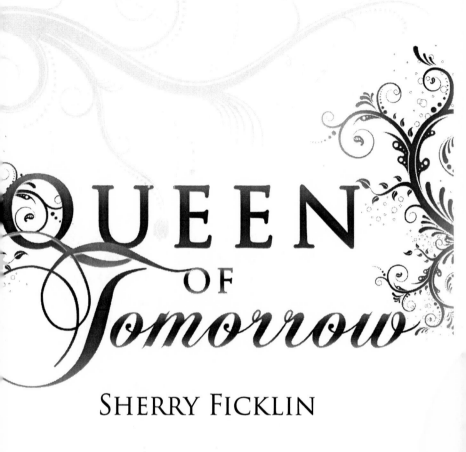

QUEEN OF Tomorrow

SHERRY FICKLIN

CLEAN TEEN PUBLISHING

QUEEN OF *Tomorrow*
Copyright ©2015 Sherry Ficklin
All rights reserved.

ISBN: 978-1-63422-070-5
Cover Design by: Marya Heiman
Typography by: Courtney Nuckels
Editing by: Cynthia Shepp

Praise for Queen of Someday:

"A must-read romance."
~USA Today

"(We) want to read this book for a third time—yes,
it's that good."
~Just Jared Jr. Book Club

"If I could rate this book more than five stars, I would.
It was INCREDIBLE."
~Kelli from Beautiful Book Chaos

"I don't know when the next book will be out but I
can guarantee it will be too long."
~Michelle (Goodreads reviewer)

"(This) book is utterly brilliant."
~Pearl from Bibliopearl Reviews

"Ficklin's writing is a marvel to read."
~Sara from Smitten Over Books

"Queen of Someday is a bright new addition to the
YA scene…"
~Bobbi (Goodreads Reviewer)

"…holy crap I loved that ending. It was perfect!"
~Eileen Lee of Book Captain Reviews

FOR MARCIA, RAY, CHRISSY, CHAD, AND
ANTHONY.
LET'S GET THE BAND BACK TOGETHER.
<3

For more information about our content disclosure, please utilize the QR code above with your smart phone or visit us at

www.cleanteenpublishing.com.

Prologue

"She is trying to break me," I say quietly, more to myself than to him. "Her cruelty knows no bounds."

"Yes, I suspect she is trying to break you," he agrees. "But you will not break. You are stronger than she is."

I shake my head. "I don't feel strong."

"I know, but you have one thing she doesn't. You have the capacity to not only love, but to love deeply and with your entire being. It's that love that makes you feel weak, but it is also love that makes you powerful. Think about it, is there anything you would not do, any length you would not go to, to protect the people you love?"

I don't have to think about it, the answer is obvious. "No."

"Then use this pain, turn it to your advantage. Make it your strength."

He's right. As soon as he says it, I feel the pain begin to twist inside me, bending into a new form—a cold, steely resolve.

From there, my course became very clear. I could

trace all my suffering back, not to Peter or my mother, but to the empress herself. And it was time she paid for my misery.

Chapter ONE

The cold wind whips across my face, tugging at my hair as I fly down the road on the back of my strong mare. Her hooves thunder across the frozen ground as we make our way through the thicket of trees and into the town square. I pull her to a stop and slide down before Lord Tucker, my royal escort, can stop me. When he finally catches up, the tall, slender man stops a few paces behind.

"Are you certain this is a good idea, Your Grace?" he asks nervously. His chestnut horse is dancing skittishly as he holds tight to the reins. "You really shouldn't be here."

Ignoring him, I toss the heavy, white fur cloak over my shoulder and unstrap the pack from the back of my mare, patting her gently.

This is one of the coldest winters we have had, or so I'm told. Even now, well into what should be spring, the relentless ice grips the countryside.

"People have long since run out of supplies, Lord Tucker. I will not see my people freeze or starve—not when there's something that can be done about it."

Over my shoulder, I hear footsteps and when I turn, I see several townsmen have come to receive the limited aid I have brought. The closest to me is an elderly, frail-looking man I know as Timothy Gaunt, the town blacksmith. He smiles warmly at me and despite his rugged appearance, his coal-smudged face, and thick, wiry grey beard, I can't help but smile back.

"He's right, Your Grace. It's dangerous for you here," one of the other men chimes in. "The fever has taken hold of half the town. You should not risk yourself."

I shrug, handing a stack of thick blankets to Gaunt. He accepts them with a grateful nod.

The man speaking approaches me next.

"You are truly an angel sent from heaven." He raises his face to Lord Tucker. "Thank you, My Lord."

Tucker nods but remains on his horse, waving for the man to come forward and take the bags from the back of his horse. I pull down two large satchels, one of rice and one of herbs from the court physician.

I hand them off to a woman, probably no older than myself, but hunched and with a thick scarf covering most of her face. The local midwife, Ana, I seem to recall.

"The physician says to boil these herbs and have the ill sip on the tea for three days or until the fever breaks."

She nods. Her eyes, like so many others in this

country, are a cold, icy blue, her skin a dull, sickly grey. When she takes the leather pouches, a gust of wind catches her scarf, and I catch sight of a splotchy, red rash on the side of her face. It could just be a fever rash, or it could be much worse.

"How are the little ones?" I ask gently. Last time we'd come, her two older boys were suffering mild frostbite and the little girl, perhaps only five years old, had taken ill.

"My boys are well, thank the Lord. But little Emelia is still…" Her voice trails off as a fat tear rolls from her eye and cuts a clean path down her cheek.

"Will you take me to her?" I ask.

Her eyes widen, but she nods. Behind me, I hear Lord Tucker mutter something so I hold my hand up, pretending I'd misheard him. "No, Lord Tucker, I must insist you remain here. Keep an eye toward the sky, lest a quick storm rolls in on us. We should not like to be trapped here with no provisions," I say, as if the thought of dismounting had ever even crossed his mind.

It's not that he's a bad man, I realize, but he is a lord. His upbringing and rank demands a certain disdain for the common people of his land. He is not outright cruel, unlike so many of the lords, and that earns him a bit of respect in my sight. Even if he is boring and pompous.

Ana leads me through the ramshackle town, down the cobblestone road, and to a small hut on the outskirts of the main square where a few huddled masses are working to retrieve buckets of water from a shallow, iced-over well. Inside the hut, lying on an old, fur blanket next to a small, stick fire hearth, the little girl shivers beneath a single torn piece of burlap cloth. Her small face is pink and shines with moisture. Kneeling beside her, I reach out and touch her cheek. The fever rages in her tiny body, that much I can tell instantly. Without thinking, I unstrap my cloak and lay it over her. After a moment, she stops shivering and relaxes beneath its warmth.

I pat her gently before slipping a large gold and emerald ring off my finger. It is one of many gifts Peter has lavished me with in attempt to make up for his bad behavior. I stand and hold it out to Ana.

She shakes her head. "No, Your Grace. I couldn't."

Taking her hand, I force it into her palm. "You can and you will. You see, someday, I would have your daughter as one of my maids at court. So think of this as an investment in my future happiness."

The gratitude in her face is so raw it's almost painful to see. So full of joy and hope. Things I haven't dared to allow myself to feel in some time.

"It should be more than enough to go buy new linens and some good porridge and meats. I expect her to be fat and smiling the next time I come through that door."

Ana looks for a moment as if she wants to throw her arms around me, and despite the risk, I might have let her. Instead, she fumbles into a deep curtsy. When I leave the humble shack and make my way back to the center of town, I feel a familiar warmth inside me, the feeling that testifies to me that I have chosen the right path, that all my sacrifices have been worth it.

Gaunt is waiting for me when I return, still holding the reins of my beautiful, black mare.

"I will return with more supplies as soon as I can," I promise.

Stepping forward, he drops to one knee. Taking the hem of my gown in his hands, he kisses it gently. "We can never repay your kindness, Your Grace," he says humbly.

I touch his shoulder gently. "You don't have to repay it, that's why it's called kindness."

He steps back and I nudge the horse forward, making swift pace back toward the palace.

The ride back to Oranienbaum is long and frigid. Between the wind biting at my skin like hundreds of needle pricks and Lord Tucker's cool indifference, the already chilly winter air is almost unbearable. I regret leaving my cloak for only a fraction of a moment, before I steel myself, bracing against the weather. That poor child needs it far more than I do.

"I still don't think you should coddle them so,"

Lord Tucker grumbles beside me. As the owner of the land the town sits on, they are his serfs—little better than slaves really. But they are also my subjects, as I sternly remind him.

"And what sort of revenue do you expect to receive from a town of dead men?" I ask more sharply than I intended. I have learned that there is a delicate balance to be maintained with the lords of the realm. We need their support, and in order to give it, they require a degree of amnesty to rule their provinces as they will. "There would be no farmers to grow the crops, no smiths to work the steel, and no laborers to work in your inns and shops. A small degree of compassion now will save you a great deal of trouble later," I assure him.

He closes his mouth, setting his lips in a hard line. Only last month an entire village to the west was stricken with Pox and every man, woman, and child perished. The town was reduced to ash as they had to burn the whole village to stop the spread. Money can only be made on land if there are serfs to work it. That argument had been the only reason I'd been able to convince him and several of the other lords to allow me to go in and provide the limited aid I could with my meager allowance.

All behind Peter's back, of course.

The heavy winter has dulled Peter's spirit and he feels increasingly caged, that much is evident by his erratic behavior. He refuses to go out, for fear of illness, so he entertains himself by holding elaborate military drills inside the great rotunda of Oranienbaum Palace. Only last week, he'd forced the regiment to march in the snow without their boots on as punishment for what he deemed a poor showing at the daily uniform inspection. Then, when half of them had gone ill from it, he'd locked himself in his room for three days, refusing to leave and allowing only his man Mikhail to join him.

It was three days of peace and solitude that I quite enjoyed, actually.

As we ride up the long, narrow path to the palace entrance, through the snow-covered mounds that will be elaborate gardens once spring finally arrives, I see Peter's steward and his good friend pacing nervously. Mikhail has been Peter's friend for years, and they even share the same sunshine-yellow hair and sharp nose. They look as though they could be related, brothers even, except for the stern frown nearly always riding across Mikhail's face that betrays his gloomy disposition.

He doesn't care for me much, but as Peter's last remaining confidant at court, Mikhail has borne an increasingly large share of the burden for keeping Peter entertained—and the strain is clearly wearing on him. This is not the first time in the past month I've found him waiting for me, desperate for me to help him calm Peter or distract him from one erratic idea or another. Today is no exception.

As I dismount and hand the reins over to the waiting steward, Mikhail places a hand out to accept my cloak as we walk inside. He sees I don't have it, and he raises an eyebrow questioningly. I shrug, and he drops his hand.

He opens his mouth to speak, but his eyes flicker past me to Lord Tucker and he pauses. Probably unsure if he should say anything or not.

"What is it now?" I ask with a deep sigh.

"He's practicing his archery in the main hall," Mikhail mutters unhappily.

I frown. I already know about the archery practice. I ordered the targets set up and the walls stripped only that morning, thinking it would be a good diversion for him while I traveled.

His voice drops to a whisper. "And he's begun using the guards as targets."

Of course he has.

I turn to Lord Tucker, who is wearing a nervous expression. Peter's antics haven't gone unnoticed by the nobles, and while no one has said anything, the fear is always present in their faces. The fear that their country might someday be ruled by a mad king. I smooth things over as best I can.

"Thank you for allowing me to accompany you today. It is wonderful to spend time with you, as always. I do hope you will stay for dinner?"

He blushes and bows. "Of course, Your Grace. How could I refuse you?" He holds out his hand and

I slip off my long glove, resting my palm in his. He brings it to his lips and brushes a ghost of a kiss across my knuckles. "Thank heavens for you, Your Grace," he says, his voice barely loud enough for me to hear.

He doesn't say more, just turns on his heel and leaves us. I turn my attention back to Mikhail, who rakes his hand nervously through his wavy, blond hair.

"Lead the way," I command.

Chapter

Two

As soon as I turn the corner into the great hall, I know something is terribly wrong. The stewards are watching from around the corner, and a line of red-and-blue guard uniforms obscure Peter from my view. In the chair nearest the wall, the court physician is tending a guard who has a long, wooden arrow protruding from his shoulder. I can tell he's trying not to make a sound even as the doctor pushes on the shaft, driving it through the wound so it can be removed from the other side. As I pass by, they both give me a look that's a mixture of relief and pity.

I pass the line and nod to the valet, who stands and loudly announces me.

"Her Grace, The Grand Duchess Catherine."

The guards shift, allowing me to pass. Peter is standing several paces away, resplendent as always in a deep blue tunic adorned with diamonds and sapphires, while one of the uniformed men stands in front of the hay target, a bright red apple on his head. The poor boy can't be more than fourteen, and he looks like he's about to vomit.

"Husband," I offer warmly, gliding over to him. "What interesting amusement you've discovered."

I pause, waiting for him to acknowledge me. But he releases the arrow before answering, narrowly missing the boy's neck. Behind me, the guards clap half-heartedly, and the young boy shuffles back into line.

"A test of wills," he says, turning to face me with a wide smile. "If a man can stand without fear before death, only then is he worthy to be in my service."

Licking my lips, I try to think of a solution. "Of course, but surely this is not such a test. I mean, your skill with the bow is legendary. They must know you would not purposely shoot them, and so there is no risk." He looks at me and blinks in confusion. I continue, "I mean, there's no way you would hit them deliberately, so it seems there is no danger at all."

I swallow. Truthfully, Peter's aim leaves a great deal to be desired, and most of his guards are well aware of the fact.

I clap my hands. "I know! What if I take the shot? Surely, there is a good chance I might miss, and then the risk of death would be much higher. What say you, husband?"

I try to keep my expression playful. Finally, he nods.

"Yes, you are quite right. Who among you is brave enough to allow the duchess to take a shot at you?"

In the line of men, a few raise their hands. Peter hands me the bow and moves to select my target. He chooses the tallest of the men and walks him to the hay bale. Then he digs around in the basket for the smallest apple he can find, only half the size of my fist. He takes a bite before setting it upon the guard's head and making his way back to me, a merry jaunt in his step.

Taking one of the arrows from the basket, I take a deep breath. Beside me, Peter wrings his hands, giddy with the prospect of me missing and accidently shooting the poor guard in the face. I draw the bow slowly until I feel my hand almost touch my cheek. I exhale, closing one eye to focus on the small, red target, and release the arrow. It flies true and in less than a heartbeat, there's a thud as the impaled apple lodges itself into the wall behind my target.

This time, the applause is genuine. Everyone looks elated and impressed. Everyone, that is, except Peter, whose face falls into a disappointed frown.

I hold up my hands for silence. "How fortunate for you that the grand duke taught me how to shoot!" I say with a laugh, and then I curtsy to Peter, who looks only slightly mollified.

"True, true," he says to the crowd. "But I tire of this. How about a new challenge?"

The guards clap again, probably in relief.

Peter takes the bow from me and glares at me with his ice-blue eyes. "Go stand in front of the target," he demands.

I hesitate for a heartbeat only, knowing that to refuse would incur his wrath. So I nod and slowly glide down the hall, replacing the guard whom I have just spared. I clasp my hands behind my back and hold my chin high. Even at this distance, I can see Peter's mind churning. He could kill me, here, in front of all these people. An accident. A game gone terribly wrong. It would leave him free to marry his mistress Elizavetta who—much to her credit—is nowhere to be seen at the moment.

A shocked murmur ripples through the onlookers. I smile widely and take an apple from the basket, resting it on my head, just behind my diamond tiara.

"Calm down, you silly people. The grand duke would never hurt me. What kind of king *accidentally* shoots his queen? He would be a laughingstock! Have faith in your future king!"

A nervous laugh reverberates through the crowd at my words.

Peter glares at me as he considers my words. When he draws the bow, I see something flicker in his eyes, and I wonder if he cares what people will think, or if being rid of me may just be worth it to him.

At the last moment, Mikhail rushes in. "Sorry to disturb you, Your Grace, but I have an urgent letter from King Frederick."

Peter lowers the bow, looking at his friend. Relief washes through me, so sudden and overwhelming that I wonder if I might actually faint from it. With a reluctant nod, he motions for me to join him, handing the bow off to his steward. Taking the apple off my head, I follow, handing it to the doctor as I pass. Before leaving the hall, I turn, clapping loudly.

"The rest of you, back to your posts. That will be enough games for today."

Peter's private study is a massive, ornate room filled with racks of books he will never read and portraits he never cares enough to look at. The walls are carved stone with gold filigree, and the floor is blanketed in a lush, hand-woven carpet with blue and gold threads intertwined to look like the night sky. In the very corner of the room stands his most prized possession, a medieval suit of armor from one of his distant ancestors.

Crossing the room, he moves behind his desk. Made of stout box maple, it's stacked high with papers he has yet to sign and orders he has yet to approve. With one grand sweep of his arm, he brushes it all off onto the floor in a heap.

He holds out his upturned hand, and Mikhail gives him the letter. Taking the long, thin knife from his hip belt, Peter slices through the wax seal with a flourish and starts to read. After staring at the pages for a few minutes, his expression set in a worried frown, he hands the letter to me.

I read the pages quickly. Peter dismisses Mikhail with a flick of his hand. Once he's gone, Peter leans forward in his chair and looks up at me.

I hand the letter back. "I don't understand," I say meekly. "The letter implies that the empress has changed sides."

Peter nods. "My aunt is ever a fickle woman. That bastard Bestuzhev must have her ear again."

I raise an eyebrow. "I don't think it's her ear he's got," I murmur, earning me a sly smile from Peter. Sometimes, in these private moments between us, when he looks at me not as a wife who has disappointed him, but as a friend, a confidant, I wonder if there could ever be love between us. Or, at least, a cessation of hostilities. Then I remember it was my own mistakes that turned him from me, my betrayal that stung him so badly he pushed me from his heart. I want to apologize, to throw myself at his feet. But he is too callous for forgiveness. I know, without a doubt, that if I ever saw fit to hand him my heart, he would crush it to dust without a moment of hesitation. And so things remain unchanged between us. But at least we have these small moments of... perhaps not friendship, but at least respect.

"You should have let me kill him when I had the chance," Peter complains.

I wish I could disagree, but I don't even open my mouth. Saving Bestuzhev after Peter savagely beat him was what secured my place in the empress' esteem. Though the man tried to kill me, he is one of her favorites. At the time, Peter's actions seemed rash and cruel, but now I see there is much more to life at court than I thought. And one of those things is the need to eliminate an enemy before they can become a threat—something I have been too softhearted to do myself.

"What are we supposed to do?" Peter demands, standing and tossing his chair aside in a fit of rage.

I bite my lip. How I wish Sergei were here. As my friend and advisor, I could use his counsel now. Never mind how much I miss him in other areas. My heart flutters at the thought. When he was called back to Winter Palace weeks ago, we assumed it was to help finalize the negotiations of the treaty between Russia and Prussia. But according to this letter, those negotiations had not just fallen through, but blown up in everyone's faces.

And I have no idea why.

Peter points to me. "Our marriage was supposed to cement the alliance with Frederick. That was the whole point of you."

I nod. It was supposed to do much more than that. It was supposed to gain King Fredrick's blessing and support for my family back in Germany. I had my title when I came to Russia a year ago, but nothing else. We were on the verge of ruin. Only my marriage to Peter, and the alliance between our countries, would save them.

I think of them now, my sweet, kind-natured father and my dear little brother, even my cold, calculating mother whose ambition alone had brought me to my current position. Will they be safe? What does this turn of events mean for them?

"What can we do?" I ask, looking at Peter.

He wipes his hand down his face. "If the treaty isn't signed yet, we can try to change her mind."

"We need to go back to St. Petersburg," I say softly.

He nods. "My aunt has a fondness for you. Perhaps if you speak with her…" He trails off.

"I will try, of course," I offer. It's true she seems to favor me over her own nephew, but the fact I have yet to provide her with the heir she so desperately needs is stretching those bonds badly. That was Peter's plan, of course. To refuse to bed me as his wife, then have me declared barren and sent away so he could marry another. I thought perhaps my tryst with Sergei would prevent such humiliation, but with him gone from me now as well, that hope is quickly dwindling.

I take a step forward, and the room around me swims. A sudden flush washes over me, and I can't catch my breath. Managing to bolt from the room just before my stomach heaves, I fall to my knees in the hall outside his door and retch all over the cool marble floor.

I have only a moment to recall the faces of those poor serfs, struck down with fever, before another wave of nausea hits me. Have I unwittingly brought sickness to the palace? I glance back over my shoulder and watch Peter, his face etched with fear, close the door between us.

Chapter

THREE

I 'm still ill the next morning, and Peter's fear is less for my well-being and more for his own, as he watches from the doorway while the doctor examines me.

"Stress," the elderly physician declares, and there is a wave of relief through the room. Peter vanishes immediately, leaving my ladies and maids to tend to me.

By the next day, I'm feeling better, though still a bit weak. I'm strong enough to visit Peter at supper, though the smells of spiced meats and cakes sits in the air like a cloud, threatening to make me retch again. I take a seat beside him, earning me a glare from his other companion.

To Peter's left is the ever-puffy Elizavetta, my one-time lady and now his mistress. Her red hair is powdered tonight, nearly as pale as her ghostly white face. Her wide, red lips are turned in a grimace as she glares at me. I take a sip of wine and try to ignore her as I turn to Peter.

"I am nearly well enough to travel," I assure him.

"When should we leave for St. Petersburg?"

Elizavetta's head snaps around, her glare moving from my face to his.

He nods, taking a quick drink of vodka. "As soon as possible. I will alert the garrison to be ready by morning."

I tilt my head in agreement.

Across from me, the red-haired girl pouts, practically laying her ample bosom on the table as she does so, attracting Peter's attention. He stares at her, regarding me with a wave of the hand.

"Two carriages," he adds. "I will take one, and you shall take the other." His eyes swing to mine. "In case your illness proves contagious."

I dip into a quick curtsy. The idea of the long ride to St. Petersburg in the same carriage as Peter is not my preference either, so I let Elizavetta think she has a victory in the matter as I rise to leave.

"I will go and oversee the packing," I offer, taking my leave.

They don't wait until I'm gone to begin pawing at each other like rabid wolves. Although I don't look back, I can hear the sounds and it pushes me over the edge. I scurry out the door and vomit again.

Stress indeed.

Once recovered, I walk slowly back to my private chamber, stopping at a small alcove near the west wall. A riot of colors dance on the cool white floor as the last rays of the sun stream through a stained-glass window. The show reminds me of another window, in another life, where I laid in the arms of a man I loved. The memory washes over me peacefully at first, then, like a shower of broken glass, begins to sting and burn, like so many ashes on my tongue.

I push the thought away.

Life at court has been strenuous, but bearable. That is due in main part to my dear, beloved Sergei. He is my champion, Lancelot to my Guinevere. It is his arms I rush to in the dark of night, his kisses I feel on my face in my dreams. My solitary respite in an otherwise dreary existence.

And right now, he's back at the Winter Palace, at the beck and call of Empress Elizabeth, and I am alone once more.

The Grand Duke and Duchess' apartments in the east wing of Oranienbaum Palace are vast and composed of two separate chambers that lead into one larger sitting room. Beyond that room, we share a massive bedchamber that is accessible through the sitting room only. It is that chamber, taken up mostly by a massive, four-poster bed draped in royal blue velvet blankets and layers of down pillows, where Peter and I are locked every night, on the empress' orders. At sunrise, the doors are opened and we rush to freedom.

As I enter my private chamber, my maids hurry to greet me like a pack of hungry pigeons at the sight of crumbs. I immediately give my orders. "The grand duke and I are leaving for St. Petersburg tomorrow. Have two carriages readied and pack our things. Maria, you will be riding with me. The rest of you will remain here and tend to the household while I'm away."

Maria beams at my words. She is stocky for a girl her age, short and a little plump with dark hair and eyes like coal. She is also the only one of my new ladies whose company I can tolerate for long periods of time, thus her enviable position as the Great Mistress of The Court. She's quiet, sweet, and mostly keeps to herself—all admirable qualities to me.

Though I know each of my ladies and their backgrounds, I try to remain distant from them. The last lady-in-waiting I allowed myself to truly befriend was Ekaterina, and she ended up married to Alexander Mananov, the man I was set to run away with before being caught by the empress. They were forced to marry to spite me, as punishment for my crimes against the empress.

I will not see such affections used against me in the future. I have nearly a dozen ladies now, though only five are regularly in attendance. My married ladies tend to spend their time in other service, and I do not begrudge them that. They join me at events here in the palace, but they won't be traveling with me.

Inwardly, I steel myself for my next order of business. Leaving my chamber, I make my way to the throne room where Peter's advisors wait.

When I enter, the men drop into deep bows as the steward announces me.

"Her Grace, The Grand Duchess Catherine."

"Gentlemen," I offer meekly. "I'm afraid the grand duke is otherwise occupied at the moment. If you would allow, I would gladly represent him at this meeting."

Across from me, they mutter. Peter hasn't attended more than a handful of meetings with his lords in the three months we've been at court, and they are rightly cross about it. Still, they also seem a bit relieved. Something tells me they don't accomplish much when he *does* bother to attend.

Lord Markus Kennith takes my hand, kissing it reverently. "We would be glad to hear your thoughts, Your Grace."

Markus is much older than I am, though you would never know it. A dedicated bachelor, he is the ruin of many a servant girl. Between his keen brown eyes and his easy charm, it's a wonder they don't simply toss themselves at him night and day. But his beauty has little effect on me, for I have held much more handsome men in my arms. I think it is for this reason he is so taken with me, that he is simply in awe of any female not stunned into silence by his every smile.

"Thank you, Lord Kennith. What is the business today?"

"Silks," Lord Keeling responds, earning him a groan from the rest of the group.

"Have your negotiations with our eastern neighbors yielded no new avenues for trade?" I ask, knowing it's not trade negotiations that keep him traveling to the Far East, but his love of adventure—and exotic women.

He shakes his head. "No, Your Grace. I think I shall have to make another trip—"

I cut him off. "Do what you must, but know that this will be the last trip the grand duke can sanction without a firm delivery of goods. Is that clear?"

He nods.

"And there is the matter of the fever in the lower villages," Markus adds.

I take a deep breath. "Yes, Lord Tucker and I went out only recently to assess the issue for ourselves."

"Iron and a good deal of our grains come from those areas. With so many ill, I fear that we here at court will soon have to begin rationing flour and other commodities." Markus leans over a small table where a royal edict to that decree sits, waiting to be signed.

Another lord objects. "We should not take such desperate measures. If we do not buy their wares, how will the people maintain their living?"

"If the situation is that dire for us, how must the townspeople be struggling to meet our orders?" I ask and receive no reply. "Most of them are too ill to work anyway. Lord Kennith is right. We will restrict our intake of those goods, though to ease the burden, I suggest the additional measure of opening the court storehouses and sending aid to those towns that are worst off. They can pay it back by replenishing the stock once they have recovered."

I look around, and the men all consent. "Good," I say flatly. "What else is there?"

The lords part, and from the back of the room, a general marches forward. I don't recognize him, but he is quite young to hold such rank and his expression is boyishly awkward as he approaches me. Under his hat, I see waves of dark curls poking out around his round face. His eyes are green like the woods and his lips full. He salutes me with a fist to his heart.

"Your Grace."

I incline my head.

"I am General Orloff of the royal guard. I have come to request..." His voice wavers.

"Go ahead," I encourage, amused by his nervousness.

He steels himself, looking away as he continues. "I would humbly request new uniforms for our garrison."

I'm unable to keep the grin from my face. "Why? Is there an issue with the uniforms you have?"

He frowns, glancing at the lords before answering. "These are of Prussian design, Your Grace, and difficult to maneuver in. We would humbly request a more traditional Russian uniform."

I feel my smile falter. The uniforms are Peter's

own design, meant to emulate the armies of the great King Fredrick, and they are ill fitting and tight, better for decoration than practical use. I know many of the officers would prefer a Russian uniform and are perturbed by Peter's love of Prussia, but to approve this request is dangerous at best. To refuse might mean angering the royal guard, also an unsafe proposition.

After a moment, I come to a conclusion. "The uniforms are the grand duke's own design. I'm sure he thought them befitting his personal guard. But I see your issue. I will have to discuss the matter with him." *In a way that doesn't damage his pride,* I add in my mind. "It might take some time to convince him, but I'm confident I can bring him to an agreement. We are leaving tomorrow for a trip to St. Petersburg. I will have a decision for you by the time we return."

The young general bows stiffly, and the fabric of his tunic strains against the gesture. "Thank you, Your Grace."

"One last thing," I say before he can leave the room. "Since we are leaving tomorrow, we will have a grand feast tonight for all the lords and visitors in court. I would like to see the guards in attendance as well. Anyone not on duty should be there in full honors."

The lords bow, and the general salutes. With a nod of my head, I turn and start toward the kitchens, to alert them of my impromptu request.

The evening is a success, despite the rushed nature of it. Long tables overflow with food and wine as the court musicians play a soft allemande. The walls are lined with the royal guard, and General Orloff leads them in a short drill for the court. Elated, Peter laughs and claps before assuming the role of military leader himself and performing a detailed uniform inspection. Each guard passes admirably. When he is finished, I stand and raise a glass.

"A toast to our honorable soldiers who protect the realm from all its foes," I say, and the rest of the guests join in. "Please, join us for the feast," I add, looking at Peter.

He agrees and in a stern voice, declares, "Company, dismissed."

The guards cheer and fill the remaining empty tables. Several lords stand and offer toasts of their own, most wishing us well on our travels. Beside Peter, Elizavetta beams proudly, as if each well wish was meant just for her. She is wearing a bright blue gown with pearls draped across the bodice, woven through her hair, and strung tightly around her neck. A bright plumage of peacock feathers sticks out of the back of her hair, making her look a bit like an overstuffed turkey. Peter leans over and kisses her deeply.

I stab a piece of meat with more force than

truly necessary and slide it around my silver plate. Somewhere deep inside, I wonder if I should have her killed. The thought is so dark and so foreign it takes me by surprise. How could I even think of such a thing? I'm not a killer. Yet, my hate for her is so deep, it feels like ichor in my veins. A poison that must be bled out.

Pushing the malignant thought aside, I stand up. My gold, brocade gown swishes around my legs as I round the table and head for the foyer. Before I can make it, however, a voice calls out.

"Grand Duchess Catherine, leaving us so soon?"

I turn and meet the pine-green eyes of young General Orloff.

"I'm afraid the meal has sat ill with me," I say gently, unable to keep myself from glancing back to my table where Peter has drawn Elizavetta into his lap and is kissing her neck.

He lowers his voice, leaning close to me. "I want you to know that I think—that is, we of the guard think—that His Grace's behavior is beyond deplorable. There is no honor in infidelity."

I smile, amused by his affronted tone. "I appreciate your indignation on my behalf. It warms my heart to know that chivalry thrives among my royal guards."

He bows. "Before you go, may I be so bold as to ask you for a dance?"

I debate the offer only for a moment before holding out my hand and letting him guide me to the dance floor. We join in a dance already in progress, and I feel something lift from my shoulders, a tension I've been holding for so long I have almost forgotten how light the world could feel without it.

He smiles a boyish smile as we step together, and then apart, spinning to and fro. When the music finally ends, we clap and he bows to me deeply. I feel the flush in my cheeks, the warmth of my skin, and for a moment, the rest of the world falls away. The general is replaced by Lord Kennith, who leads me in another dance. Soon, my face aches from laughing so hard as he whispers various jokes into my ear every time we pass close.

"…and the general responds, *lad, I only meant for you to ride him into town*," he whispers, finishing a particularly inappropriate yarn.

I laugh, and my side aches from it. The dance ends and another lord takes his place, then another soldier. Before I know it, the sky beyond the windows is glowing with the first rays of morning's pale light. I look around and see the hall is nearly empty. Peter has fallen asleep in his plate and is snoring loudly next to a very drunk Elizavetta, who has her chin propped up on her fist and is glaring at me while fighting to keep her eyes open.

It's Mikhail who takes my hand next, not to dance but to lead me away from the floor. As we exit, a group of people groans behind us. I glance over my shoulder and wave. "Another evening, gentlemen," I say playfully, letting Mikhail escort me off the floor and down the hall toward my chamber.

"You seemed happy tonight," he says out of nowhere.

I glance over, but he is staring to the front, his expression unreadable. I say nothing, and the silence between us grows uncomfortably. Mikhail, always Peter's best man, never particularly cared for me, and I have no reason to think that his opinion of me has changed.

"That's good," he finally adds. "It's nice to see you smile again."

Now I frown. He has never spoken two kind words to me, yet here he is, expressing pleasure at my joy. It feels very insincere somehow. "I can find the chamber on my own. You should see to Peter," I say curtly.

He stops, turns to me, and bows. "Of course, Your Grace. I only meant…" He doesn't finish the thought. Instead, he shakes his head and walks away, leaving me in the empty hallway.

By the time I get to my room, the sun has risen over the hills and shines in the windows brightly as the maids busily pack the trunks.

"The carriages will be ready in less than an hour," Maria says with a curtsy.

There's just enough time for the maids to help me wash and change before they arrive. Once I'm clean, my hair brushed out and rolled into tall curls atop my head, and I'm in my simple grey-and-silver riding gown, I return to the main chamber where the footmen are carrying the trunks down to the carriage. Peter is sitting in the high-backed green velvet chair near the corner of the room, shielding his eyes from the sunlight with one hand while holding a bottle of wine in the other.

"Are you feeling ill, husband?" I ask, unable to keep the amusement from my voice.

He groans. "You certainly made a spectacle of yourself last night, *wife*." He draws out the last word as if it's a vile thing on his lips.

"You had found your amusement elsewhere for the evening," I say with more venom in my voice than I intend. Then I sigh. "If you don't wish for me to dance with others, perhaps you could dance with me," I offer.

He laughs, as if it the most ridiculous thing he's ever heard. "Dance with whomever you want; it makes no difference to me."

"As you wish," I say blandly, picking up the tiara he had given me during my first week at court and setting it onto my head. Next, I carefully lift a thin, gold chain with a fire-red ruby hanging from the middle. Another of Peter's many gifts. I'm not sure why he still gives them to me, now that things are so strange and unhappy between us, but he does. Almost weekly and without fail.

Reaching behind me, I fumble with the clasp. I hear him set down his bottle and stand, crossing the room to me. Not sure of his intentions, I freeze, watching his reflection in my mirror. He walks up behind me, taking the chain in his slender hands. My heart pounds. For a moment, I'm afraid he's going to jerk the chain and choke me with it, but he doesn't. Fastening the clasp, he releases it, letting the large stone slip down onto my chest and rest there. He looks at me in the mirror and, for a heartbeat, his face softens. With one hand, he reaches up and tucks a piece of stray hair behind my ear, his fingertip just grazing my cheek as he does. I take a deep breath, terrified to move, but unable to pry my eyes off his reflection. For a moment, the briefest, most flickering of moments, I think he might lower his face and kiss me.

Peter hasn't kissed me in a very, very long time. While the thought of it once filled me with dread, all I can think now is how nice it would be to actually be loved by my husband. I let myself relax, my shoulders fall, and I look down, turning my face to his before looking back up at him from under my lashes. Then I see it in his eyes, the raw, unrestrained desire to take me in his arms. I've seen the look before, but never on his face—at least not when he was looking at me.

Chapter
FOUR

J ust then, Elizavetta bursts through the door and rushes to Peter with a high-pitched giggle, throwing herself into his arms. He recovers himself quickly, snatching her up and twirling her around. I watch them in the mirror, part of me envious, the other, darker part, telling me again that I should have her smothered in her sleep.

We load the carriages slowly. Maria brings a basket of food and a huge stack of books for the journey, and while I'm grateful for both, all I want to do is sleep. The previous evening's entertainments coupled with my constant stress and worry has left me exhausted. Once the horses are off, it doesn't take long for the soft rocking of the carriage to lull me off to sleep.

It takes a little over a day to arrive in St. Petersburg. Though the journey is relatively quick, my muscles ache. We rode through the night and into the next day. As we approach the golden gates of the Winter Palace, I peek my head out and see that the empress has assembled a grand welcome complete with guards, nobles, and musicians. Peter's carriage arrives before mine.

"Their Graces, The Grand Duke Peter and The Grand Duchess Catherine," the steward announces.

The door to my carriage is thrown open, and the valet holds out his hand to me. I let him help me out of the carriage and down the tiny step stool. Beside me, Peter does the same. I walk over to him just as Elizavetta steps out of her carriage, unaided. Peter holds out his arm, and I take it. I can practically feel the rage radiating off her as she follows behind us, Maria at her side. The scowl on Empress Elizabeth's face fades as we approach her. I don't know whether she's upset to not see me round with child or if the fact that we'd taken separate carriages bothered her, but either way, I'm sure we will hear about it soon enough.

Together, we address the empress, Peter with a bow and me with a curtsy.

"Welcome back to Winter Palace," she says loudly. "I hope your journey was without incident."

"Quite, Your Majesty," I say warmly.

"We had to take separate carriages, the duchess has been quite ill," Peter adds, withering under her stern glance.

She raises a slender eyebrow. Though she has gained some weight since the last time I saw her, the empress looks much the same. Her hair is powdered white and tall upon her head, and she is draped in so many jewels you can barely see her elaborate gown, only bits of royal blue fabric peeking out. She holds herself tall, chin high as she looks over us.

"Is that so?" she asks. I nod, and she snaps her fingers. "Fetch the physician."

"We have already seen our own physician, Your Majesty. He assures us it's nothing serious," I say quietly.

She frowns. "Well, all the same. Come, we have much to talk about." She turns, and we follow her to her private study. When we enter the room, she sits behind her massive oak desk. Flanking her on either side are Chancellor Bestuzhev and Sergei. Though Bestuzhev offers me a faint smile, I don't look at him. My eyes are locked onto Sergei. His square jaw is shadowed with stubble, his eyes dark like pools of midnight as his lips twitch up at the sight of me. It's all I have in me not to run to him and throw myself into his arms, to tell him how miserable I've been in his absence, and let him kiss me until all the darkness is driven away. But I hold my feet firmly in place, even as my heart jumps into my throat.

When I can finally look away, I see Bestuzhev still bears the scars from Peter's torture. Thin, red ridges crisscross his face and neck. One day, they will fade to white, but now, they still look fresh, as if at any moment they might split back open. His eyes are fixed on me, probably to avoid looking at Peter. I frown at him.

"Your timing is unfortunate," she begins. "I have a guest arriving tomorrow. Empress Maria Theresa of Austria is coming with her envoy."

"Why are you siding with Austria?" Peter demands. "Prussia has been our ally for decades. Why have you turned you back on King Fredrick now?"

"There are those who fear more Prussian influence in Russia. We are a sovereign state and should not be so closely tied to his causes." She pauses. "Also, I believe the change of Austrian succession should be honored. Aligning ourselves with Austria and her allies will send a message to the rest of the world that we are not just a toy in the hands of Prussia. And, of course, there are lands to be gained and gold to be paid for our loyalty."

"What changed your mind?" I ask as kindly as I can. "It has to be about more than land and gold."

She slams her fist down on the table. "Perhaps if my own dynasty were more secure, I would not have to think of such things, but I cannot side with those who would violate the laws of succession when my own hangs so feebly in the balance." She points at me, and then Peter. "I need an heir. And in that, you have failed me, both of you."

Sergei steps forward, speaking gently. "They have only been married a short time. Perhaps if we are patient, a child will come."

She stands up, enraged now. "I cannot afford to wait and hope. This alliance is my best chance to secure my throne and ensure the continuation of the Romanov line."

Her face is twisted in anger and a hint of madness. I know that she's prone to fits of instability, I've seen it before. But this is worse.

"Get out, both of you. And Peter," she calls him back, "if I so much as hear a rumor that you are bedding anyone other than your wife while you are here, I will have your little redheaded mistress strung up in the courtyard and flogged. Is that clear?" His face freezes. I can't help but wonder if she's ever spoken to him that way in her entire life.

"Yes, Your Majesty."

And with that, we leave. I shoot Sergei a quick, parting glance, but he's busy pulling the empress into his arms. My stomach twists into knots at the sight. I knew they had been lovers once, but I'd assumed when we met that all that had changed. I feel my face harden into a frown.

"She's lost her mind," Peter rages as soon as the door closes behind us. I take his arm and lead him down the hall to a small alcove.

I shake my head. "She usurped the throne from her sister. She's terrified to lose it to someone else."

"To whom?"

"Let me ask you this. If she dies, and you have no heir, your loyalty would be to King Fredrick, right? It would all but make Russia nothing but an extension of Prussia."

"He would never invade us. We are allies."

"That only holds as long as there is a balance of power. She's right, until the dynastic line is established, Russia could be easy prey for Prussia, if it should turn its mind to such a thing."

He shakes his head. "You know Fredrick. He would never do that."

I take a deep breath. "No, I don't believe he would. But if Russia is seen as weak, vulnerable, there are many who would like to see the empire collapse."

"Austria, for one. I think I may know of a way to ferret out the truth behind her change of temperament."

I raise one eyebrow. "What are you thinking?"

He looks away, his expression distant as thoughts form in his head. "I dare not say yet, but leave this matter to me."

I agree, unable to do anything else. "Then I shall go for a ride, if you don't mind. The sunshine and fresh air will do me good, I think."

He waves me off. "Yes, yes. Fine. But see the physician first, or she will be none too pleased with you."

"I will, and Peter, what she said about Elizavetta..."

He looks at me again, his face a blank mask.

"I know you truly care for her. And I know how unhappy you would be if something happened to her. So please, be discreet."

Peter chuckles dryly. "That is something I certainly never expected to hear from you."

I shrug. I've long past quit caring about his affair, though his choice of playmate still manages to infuriate me. I wonder, only briefly, if it might be easier to stomach if he were with someone I liked, or at least, was able to tolerate. "Love can be dangerous. Especially here."

His expression turns serious, and he nods once before turning his back to me. I'm about to walk away when he turns back, takes me by the shoulders, and pulls me forward unexpectedly. He hesitates for a moment before kissing me chastely on the cheek. "Until later, wife."

I'm so stunned I just stand there and watch him trot off.

I haven't been in this room since after my wedding night, when the court physician confirmed that the marriage had been consummated. The walls are lined with shelves, some holding massive tomes, others with various-sized mortar and pestles, vials of liquid, and dry herbs. The physician is an elderly man with a long, white beard and soft eyes. Though I know his name, it always escapes me. Seeing me, he bows deeply.

"What can I do for you, Your Grace?" he asks.

"I've been ill. There's a fever passing through Oranienbaum and the empress worries for me."

He motions for me to sit down, and I obey. Placing

a cone to my chest, he listens to my heart. "Have you had a fever?" he asks.

"No. Dizziness and ill stomach."

"Anything else?"

I shake my head. "No. I think it's just exhaustion. I've been very tired of late."

"That's probably all it is then. When was your last course?"

The question takes me aback. Mentally, I try to remember. "About six weeks ago. But that doesn't mean much. They never seem to come regularly for me."

He nods, turning his back to me. Pulling out a drawer in his tall bureau, he shuffles around until he finds a small vial of clear liquid. He holds it out to me. "Here, smell this."

"Smell it?" I ask, making sure I've heard him correctly. He grins sheepishly.

With a shrug, I pull the cork from the bottle and lower my nose to it. I don't even inhale before the scent hits me and I nearly fall off the chair. The vomit comes too quickly for me to hold back, and the physician manages to get a pan under my chin just in time.

"What is that?" I ask when I can finally catch my breath.

He re-corks it. "Essence of Orange. It is well known to soothe those suffering with stomach illness, though a bit overpowering for you, it seems."

"What does that mean?" I ask.

He looks at me flatly. "It means, my dear, that you are not ill. More likely, you are with child."

I stare at him blankly. "That's not possible. I haven't…" I pause, deciding how to proceed. "That is, since my last, encounter, my course has come and gone."

He shrugs. "It's not uncommon for a woman to still have a cycle even though she is early with child."

My head swims, and I feel as though I might faint. "But my physician in Oranienbaum said it was stress."

"He is probably young and has never seen this. It is rare, and you must be careful, especially so. The bleeding could mean other problems. We will just have to watch you closely."

My hands go to my stomach involuntarily. I hadn't been with anyone since the night before Sergei left, and when my course came after he was gone, I had given up hope. Could this be real? This would be the answer to so many problems. I'm so stunned that I don't know what to do next. Beside me, the physician laughs.

"This is good news, child. Don't look so shocked. Now you just have to hope it's a boy."

His words echo inside my skull, but I'm too numb to process them.

Sergei. I need to tell Sergei. As the father, I think he should know first. Then I will tell Peter and the empress.

Peter. I'd tricked him on our wedding night into thinking we'd been together when we had not. The difference would be weeks only. He would never know the child wasn't his. Sergei and I are the only ones who would know the truth.

He will be so happy. When I finally get to my feet, I want to run to him. Then a thought stops me, chilling the blood in my veins.

He's with the empress. Are they together? Is he lying with her again? Are they in each other's arms even at this very moment?

My heart sinks in my chest. I try to convince myself that it doesn't matter. He's my friend, my lover, but perhaps, I had never truly captured his heart, not the way she had—

I push those thoughts aside. I can't afford them now. I can't afford to let jealousy or hurt upset what I have sacrificed so much for. A child.

I find myself wandering the halls, though I'm not sure where my feet are taking me. I end up outside a familiar door. I stare at it for a moment, not brave enough to go inside. Though Alexander is long gone, his memory haunts me. Once, I thought to marry him, to feel his child turning in my womb, but that fate went to another. I chose my path, and I cannot shrink from it now.

Heading for my chamber, I decide to change into my habit and go for that ride. The fresh air will do me good and help me clear my mind before I tell the empress the news tonight. There will be a feast and a ball, as there always is, and I'm sure some kind of theater. I must tell her the news before Empress Maria Theresa arrives from Austria, before that treaty can be signed.

I change quickly and head for the stables, never expecting what I will find there.

Chapter
FIVE

Night is falling quickly, and I know my ride must be a short one. When I reach the stable of my favorite mare, Peony, I find someone else already saddling her.

"General Orloff?" I ask, unsure of my own eyes.

He turns to me, a wide smile on his face. He bows and places his fist over his chest. "Your Grace," he responds.

"What are you doing here?"

"I ride with your personal guard," he answers.

I feel worry creep into my mind. This young man should not be here, and I instantly wonder what his motives are. "But General Franz is the head of my personal guard. Where is he?"

He shakes his head. "Franz stayed behind in Oranienbaum. I took his place."

I chew my bottom lip. "Why would you do that?" My tone is an accusation, although I try to keep it light. For the first time in some weeks, fear rushes in like ice in my veins. Does he mean me harm, this handsome young soldier?

He shifts nervously, handing me the reins. "May I speak freely?"

I tense, unable to stop myself. My hands ball into fists as I prepare to fight him off. "Of course."

When he speaks, I feel myself relax even as my surprise at his candor shakes me.

"I see your unhappiness, and I see the way the grand duke treats you. I know how sad and alone you must feel. Yet you are by far the kindest, bravest, cleverest woman I have ever had the pleasure to meet. The way you handle the lords, the kindness you show to the serfs, these things make you a true ruler. I would, if you will have me, serve as your personal guard. I will watch over you at all times and against all enemies, even those who might have a crown upon their heads," he adds in a deep voice.

He drops to one knee and lowers his head. "I swear to you my loyalty and my fealty, above all others. I will be your sword and your shield. Please, do me this honor."

I'm so touched by the gesture I can hardly speak. To swear fealty to me, above Peter, and above even the empress herself, is a dangerous thing. Treason at the very least. And yet, how could I possibly refuse? The idea of having him in my corner is far too tempting.

I touch the side of his head gently. "I would be honored to have you guard me. I accept your pledge and make a pledge of my own. I swear that I will strive to be worthy of your loyalty and the trust that you have placed in me."

When he looks up at me, there is fierceness in his expression. He has made a vow to me and in that moment, I know he will keep it—no matter the cost. His resolution is like the sun on his face—he could not hide it if he tried.

He stands. "Then let me begin by escorting you during your ride."

I nod. He helps me onto Peony before mounting his own horse. I plan on taking it easy tonight, but realize it might be the last chance I have to ride, once news of the pregnancy gets out, so I decide to let her run.

My young guard stays close, but still keeps a respectable distance as we fly over the low brush and through the trees, making a wide circle to the river and back.

When we return to the stables, the groom is there to take the horses and Orloff follows me back to my chamber, taking up his position outside my door. I am almost inside when I pause, looking back at the young man standing tall in his blue-and-red uniform.

"What is your name?" I ask curiously. "Your full name."

"Grigori Stanislaw Orloff, Your Grace."

"Thank you, Grigori," I say informally. He bows, and I close the door between us.

When I emerge from my chamber again, Marie has helped me into a lovely, pale pink gown with red sleeves and Spanish lace. I make my way to Sergei's private chambers. When he opens his door, he smiles widely and nearly reaches for me before seeing my guard at my back.

"Sergei, I must speak with you. Do you have a moment?"

He licks his lips and nods, holding his door open enough for me to slip in.

"General, please wait for me here. I will only be a moment."

If Grigori suspects anything improper, he says nothing, nor does his expression falter. Only once I'm in the room and Sergei closes the door does he rush to me. Lifting me into his strong arms, he kisses me ferociously.

"Oh, Sophie, how I have missed you," he says, his voice husky.

Anyone else I would correct. Catherine is my name now. But something about the way *Sophie* rolls off his tongue in his thick Russian accent makes me shiver, so I let it pass. I take his face in my hands and when his lips wander down to kiss my chest, I pull his face back up, bringing his lips back to mine.

"And I you. But I have news, wonderful news."

He leans back but never releases me, his arms still coiled around my waist. It's I who has to step back, breaking the embrace.

"I am with child," I say softly.

His expression is one of disbelief that quickly fades into a radiant smile. Stepping forward, he takes my hands. "My child?"

I nod. "Our child."

He drops to one knee and rests his forehead against my belly. "It's a miracle," he whispers, kissing my stomach.

"Are you happy?" I ask. "Truly? I know that no one can know the child's true paternity—"

He stops me with a kiss. "Of course I'm happy. You are going to have my child. My son will be the emperor of Russia. What a beautiful gift you've given me." He clutches me to him, kissing the side of my face and into my hair. "I love you, Sophie, with all my heart and soul, I love you."

"We need to go tell the empress the good news," I say softly, hesitant to let go of him, but knowing I must.

He nods. "Of course."

"And Peter," I say.

He nods again, bringing my hands to his lips and kissing them reverently. "You and I will celebrate later," he whispers with a sly grin that I can't help but return.

Making our way from his chamber and down the hall, we run into Peter and Mikhail. They are deep in discussion and nearly barrel into me.

"Peter," I say happily, "Just who I was looking for. I need to speak to the empress. Would you be so kind as to join me?"

He looks stupefied by my request but recognition quickly registers on Mikhail's face.

"I will take care of everything, Your Grace," he says, releasing Peter to me with a bow.

"What is it?" Peter asks as Sergei falls in step behind us.

"A surprise," I say, unable to keep the smile off my face.

"I hate surprises," Peter mutters as we arrive and ask the steward to announce us.

When we are motioned in, the empress is in a new gown, this one with the widest pannier I've ever seen. I wonder how she will be able to maneuver in the thing, much less sit or any other simple task. Her hair is jet black, feathers towering out the very top, making her look freakishly tall.

"Your Majesty, I bring news from the physician. He says I am with child," I say loudly. I feel Peter turn beside me, facing me in disbelief. It takes her a moment to respond, as if she's not entirely certain she heard me correctly. But as soon as my words settle in, a wide grin spreads across her face. I glance out of the corner of my eye and see Peter frozen, his lips parted, a look of disbelief etched into his features.

"You stupid girl, how did you not know sooner?"

she demands, her voice playful.

I lower my chin. "I've never been with child before. It seems I did not know the symptoms."

Laughing, she rushes over to me, nearly knocking Bestuzhev out of the way as she moves past him. She pulls me into a tight embrace before quickly releasing me.

"Oh, this is wonderful, just wonderful," she squeals in delight.

"Is it true?" Peter whispers beside me.

I turn to face him fully, unsure what his reaction will be, and I am instantly hit with a wave of guilt. His face looks so stunned, yet somehow, serene. I've never seen him wear such an expression. He hesitantly reaches out and flattens his palm against my belly.

"Will it be a boy?" he asks, his voice soft.

"I don't know," I say honestly. "I hope so."

He sighs deeply. "A son. I'm going to be a father."

I bite my bottom lip as the truth threatens to explode from inside me. All I can do is nod for fear of what might escape my mouth should I open it.

The corner of his mouth picks up in a half grin. When he looks up at me again, there is a light in his eyes that I've never seen before. "And you, Little Mother. We are going to have a son."

I swallow the jagged lump that's formed in my throat. I think this is the first time in months that he has looked at me with anything less than veiled disdain. But his expression is joyous, radiant as the noonday sun. I have to admit, this is not the reaction I expected, considering his plan to have me declared barren and set aside. Yet he stands before me, happier than I have seen him—possibly ever—and it makes me happy too. His smile—when genuine—is truly contagious.

"We need to celebrate," he says with a thunderous laugh. "And you can call off your ridiculous treaty with Austria."

The empress exchanges a look with Bestuzhev that makes me think it might not be an option any longer, but Peter doesn't see it. He's busy staring at me excitedly.

"What do you think, Little Mother? What will we name him?"

"Peter, perhaps," the empress interrupts. "Or Paul. Yes, Paul I should think."

"Of course," I comply easily.

"Who is this?" Peter asks, finally noticing Grigori standing in the back of the room.

"He's my personal guard. I brought him in as soon as I got news of the pregnancy," I lie smoothly.

"Good thinking," the empress says thoughtfully. "We can't be too careful now, can we?"

"Don't worry, I won't let you out of my sight from this moment on," Peter promises, taking my hand.

I balk at the gesture, but he doesn't seem to notice.

I'd forgotten how possessive Peter could be with things he felt belonged to him. This child would be no different. I spare a glance over my shoulder to Sergei, wondering how on earth I am going to find a way past Peter to visit him. The idea of not being in Sergei's arms for the next eight months is enough to make my chest ache.

"We will make the announcement at dinner tonight," the empress declares.

Somehow, her generous chamber begins to feel very small, and I can't seem to catch my breath.

"I think the grand duchess is a bit overwhelmed. Perhaps she could use some fresh air before the celebration tonight?" Sergei says, completely in tune with exactly what I need, as always.

"I'll take her outside," Peter says quickly, leading me out the door before anyone can stop him. Sergei and Grigori follow behind us. Peter walks with one hand at the small of my back, the other protectively in front of my stomach. It's so strange I almost laugh.

That is, until we turn the corner and run into a very pink-faced Elizavetta. She sees Peter's gesture and immediately flies into a rage. Stepping forward, Peter places himself between her and me, taking the brunt of her attack. There's a sharp *whap* as she slaps Peter across the face. I can tell from her expression that she instantly regrets it, but it's too late. Peter grabs her arm and backhands her, sending her sprawling to her knees on the hard floor. He draws back to hit her again and she whimpers, shielding her face with her free hand.

"Don't you ever even think of harming my wife or my child ever again, do you hear me?" he screams, releasing her arm violently.

She nods, tears rolling down her round cheeks, but he just steps past her, taking hold of me once more.

"Come along, Little Mother. Let's get you some air and something to drink," he says protectively.

I can't help but to watch her over my shoulder as I'm ushered down the hall. She's sitting in a crumpled heap, her face red and blotchy, blood trickling from her nose and mouth, and for the first time ever, I understand what it means to be loved by Peter.

And I'm well and truly afraid.

Chapter
Six

Though the air outside is crisp against my skin, it does nothing to calm my nerves. Peter hovers over me, much too close for any kind of comfort, while Sergei looks on. I have to give him credit; he manages to keep his expression neutral, despite whatever emotions are raging beneath his calm exterior.

Grigori stands stone-faced at the door, his alert eyes never leaving me.

I've never felt quite so much like a bird in a cage.

Soon enough, Peter begins to fuss, bored by just standing there, and suggests we go inside. I comply but before I can make it into the hallway, I see that he's stopped behind me, turning to Sergei.

"There will be no further need of your services today, General," Peter barks.

Sergei bows, his eyes flickering up to me briefly. I nod almost imperceptibly and he takes his leave of us, heading back toward the empress' apartments. Once he's gone, Peter turns his attention back to me.

"Are you hungry? Thirsty?" he asks softly, taking

my hand in his.

I shake my head, unable to hold my tongue any longer. "Peter, why the sudden change of heart?" I ask, adding quickly, "Not that I'm ungrateful for your kindness. It just seems very sudden."

He wets his lips with his tongue before answering, never raising his eyes to mine. "My father died when I was very young. Some days, I struggle to remember what his face looked like, and I realize the only images of him I can recall are from paintings I've seen."

He pauses, shifting uncomfortably before continuing. "When Aunt Elizabeth named me her heir, I thought I would finally have family. But it was a hollow wish. She never truly cared for me. I was nothing but a male to carry on the family name, a pawn in her bid to keep control of the empire."

When his bright blue eyes finally find mine, they are glistening with pain. "Even here, surrounded by people, I was always utterly alone. At least until Mikhail and Alexander came. They were my only friends in this place. Then you came and I thought that you would be mine, that you would be the one person here to truly love me, but you chose him. You gave your heart to him, and then you drove him from me."

His voice edges toward anger at the end of his words, but then he sighs deeply and I watch all that rage fall away.

I squeeze his hand. "I'm sorry. I know that isn't

enough, not even close to enough, but I am truly sorry," I say gently.

He blinks, shaking his head. "It doesn't matter now. Now I will have our son, and he will love me. He will love us both and through him, I will have my family."

He steps back and holds out his arm, which I accept, and I let him lead me back to our rooms. Though the trip is a silent one, his words weigh heavily on my heart. I have only ever thought of this child as a way to please the empress. I never realized how much it would mean to him. The guilt of the truth weighs on me like a stone on my chest. What will he do if he discovers the truth? I suddenly feel the world around me, fragile as a spiderweb made of glass, and I know how carefully I must tread now.

The banquet is alive, bursting with the boisterous revelry of the guests. Musicians play merry songs and course after course of food is heaped upon the long tables before us. Even Mikhail is smiling, a look unbecoming of him. I don't realize why he's smiling until at one point, he leans across the table and whispers to me.

"Congratulations on the happy news."

Though the empress hasn't made an official statement yet, Peter is spreading the word to anyone within hearing distance. He's also downing glass after glass of wine, and while I normally discourage that behavior, tonight I just smile. Let him have his celebration. Let him drink until he passes out cold on the stone floor, and we have to drag him into bed. That will only serve to make my escape into Sergei's chamber that much easier.

There are so many noble guests in attendance, and the always glittering empress goes out of her way to flirt and fawn over each of them in turn, especially the handsome ones. Now, she is sitting beside Prince Edward, Duke of York and cousin to the king of England. Her tall hair is falling to the side, just a bit, and he keeps hiding his face with his hand as he tries not to laugh. He is certainly attractive, all black hair and boyish dimples, and while she laughs deeply at something he's said, he shoots me a look of desperation.

Standing slowly, I make my way over to introduce myself.

Seeing me coming, he stands, bowing from the neck, while at the empress' left, Chancellor Bestuzhev introduces me.

"Of course, she needs no introduction, my good man. Word of her beauty and grace has reached even the far away coast of England. Your Grace, I am so pleased to make your acquaintance," he says, taking my hand and grazing a chaste kiss across the back of my hand.

"And I yours," I respond softly. "Tell me, what brings you to court?"

He looks down, and then back up sheepishly. "Ah, well, I wish I could say it was a strictly recreational visit, but I am here doing business on behalf of my king."

"I see. You are here about the treaty with Austria."

He smirks, lifting only the corner of his thin lips. "Among other things. Would you care to dance?"

Beside me, the empress begins fanning herself with a scrap of lace and leans over to whisper something to the chancellor.

"Of course," I say pleasantly and allow him to lead me to the dance floor.

As the music begins, a slow allemande, we begin to sway. "It's very clever, you know," I say as we pass closely to each other before being drawn back into line.

"What's that?" he asks.

"Sending you to negotiate on behalf of the king. The last envoy lacked the, ah... charm necessary to capture the empress' attention."

He chuckles. "So I have heard. Do you think me charming, then?"

Now it's my turn to smirk. "I think you are well practiced in capturing the attentions of women."

"And have I captured your attention?" he asks boldly.

I take his hand as we stroll down the procession

line. "My support, perhaps. I dislike the idea of a treaty with Austria; I think you feel the same. My attention, however, is solely focused on other matters at present."

"I take that as a challenge," he says playfully.

"You shouldn't," I respond flatly. "You have your part to play here, as do I. For the moment, our political interests, at least, are aligned. I would suggest you return your attentions to flattering the empress, for all the charm in the world would be wasted on me."

"Are you so deeply devoted to your husband?" he asks boldly, looking me square in the eye. "Or is there a much sadder reason behind your indifference?"

His words are like a blast of cold water pouring over me. Before I can say anything else, the empress stands, raising her hand for the music to stop, and then bellows loudly.

"I am so very happy to announce to you, my friends and allies, that the grand duke and duchess are expecting a child."

The room erupts in applause and cheers. Across the room, where Peter sits half upright in his chair, he raises his glass of wine, sloshing a little over the rim so it dribbles onto his jacket.

"Congratulations," the prince manages before Empress Elizabeth bursts between us.

"You, my dear, should probably not be dancing so. All that bouncing can't be good for the baby. And while I'm thinking about it, that dress isn't the best idea either."

I look down at my white gown. It's simple, but the lace is soft and flowing, and it perfectly contrasts my dark hair and eyes. "What's wrong with it?" I ask before I can think better of it.

"The corset is too tight and the bodice too low. Until the child comes, you should really wear loose-fitting garments. I can have some sent to your rooms in the morning. For now, why don't you take Peter and go get some rest? We wouldn't want to tire you." She practically growls the words before turning to Edward, her entire tone changing.

"If you are looking for a dancing partner, I would be happy to oblige," she says meekly. He takes her hand, shooting me a glance over her shoulder that's a mix of understanding and pity.

I shake my head, motioning for Mikhail to retrieve Peter, and then I head for my room as instructed, with my young general at my heels.

No sooner do I arrive than Mikhail and Sergei burst into the room with a stupefied Peter in tow. He's barely able to hold himself upright as they walk him to the settee. His head lolls back, and he looks at me blissfully.

"Hello, Little Mother," he offers with a wide, intoxicated grin. Then his head rolls forward again, and he lifts one leg. "I seem to have lost a shoe."

The missing footwear sends him into a fit of laughter and he rolls off the velvet couch and spills onto the floor, his chuckles quickly changing into soft snores.

I shake my head, waving for the men to take him. "Help the grand duke into bed. I will be there shortly," I say, unable to keep the joy from my voice.

Once he's in bed, Mikhail and Sergei bow before me. Sergei raises his eyes into a questioning glance before turning to take his leave. Mikhail follows behind and Grigori closes my door, no doubt taking up his position outside my room.

I shake my head and let my ladies help me into my nightgown. Though it is still cold outside, I throw open the windows to my room. Partly to stir the air and also to help rid the area of the stench of alcohol clinging to my sheets. From the bed, Peter stirs, rolling onto his stomach.

"Don't hate me," he murmurs into the pillow before falling back to sleep.

His words, so childlike, so raw and exposed, kindle something inside me. It's small, a subtle warmth that wells up in my belly and floods through my veins.

Crossing the room, I pull the thick damask blankets up over him, just staring at him for a few moments. Reaching out, I stroke a wispy, yellow curl back from his face. So many emotions battle inside me, the strongest, fiercest of them all, is a deep, aching regret. Regret for what might have been. My hand hovers over his face and for the first time, I hesitate, wondering how I've allowed myself to wander so far off the course I sought out to tread. Finally, he snores once and rolls over, tucking his face into the pillow. Retreating from the bedside, I retrieve a book from my shelf and settle into the seat by the window to read for a while. When I look up from the pages some time later, the candles beside me have melted nearly in half and I can no longer hear the music playing floors below. The palace, much like Peter, has fallen into silence.

Setting the book on the table, I quickly don my long, white cloak, step into the bath chamber, and push open the small, hidden door leading to the kitchen. Sergei had directed me to it, not long after the wedding, and it was well used until our departure. Unlike the nights in Oranienbaum, there is no one to lock Peter and me into our rooms—and no reason to do so now. I slip down the narrow stairs and into the kitchen without making a sound, my feet bare and cold against the stone floor. I quickly make my way down the hall to the wing where Sergei's room lies.

When I turn a corner, I abruptly come upon two men. I duck into the shadows before they see me and hold my breath as they talk. One I recognize immediately as the charming Prince Edward. The other is a nobleman by the name of Ivanovitch. I have met him before, and though he is tall and slender, always a smile on his face, he set me ill from the first moment. Something about him, something I could not begin to explain, had always given me a feeling as though he was not to be trusted.

"She arrives tomorrow. By the next sunrise, the deed will be done," he assures Edward.

"And there will be no way to trace it back to us?"

Ivanovitch claps a hand on his shoulder. "You worry too much."

I watch as Edward brushes his hand away with disdain. "And you do not worry enough."

The two men go their separate ways, leaving the hallway empty before me.

I rap lightly on Sergei's door, and it flies open. He pulls me inside with one arm around my waist.

Once the door is closed behind me, I throw myself into his arms, kissing him fiercely, all my tension and worry melting away in the feel of him pressed against me. I run my hand along his jaw, enjoying the feel of his whiskers across my fingertips. When I finally pull back, I see a need in his blue-green eyes, raw and masculine. His face is flushed, his lips full, as he weaves his fingers into my hair with one hand and with the other, expertly unties the cord around my neck, letting my cloak fall to the floor at my feet.

I want to stop him, to tell him what I have just overheard, but I'm too lost in the moment to get the words out. When he reaches down, scooping me off my feet and into his arms, I can't help but relax against him, letting the world slip completely away.

As we lie tangled in his soft, white sheets, my head nestled into his chest, I sigh contentedly. He traces tiny circles in the small of my back with the tip of his finger, sending goosebumps along my exposed skin.

"How are you feeling?" he asks.

I stretch, kissing his bare chest. "Better now," I say honestly.

He chuckles. "I mean the baby."

The sides of my mouth perk up. "Fine. A little ill at times, but nothing I can't suffer."

"Peter seems excited by the prospect," he says absently.

I nod. "It surprised me, to be honest." Turning, I raise my chin and stretch up, kissing him full on the lips. "Sometimes, we don't realize how badly we want something, until we have it," I add softly, tracing his lips with my fingertips. He seizes them and kisses them gently.

"Prince Edward certainly seemed taken with you this evening," he says, changing the subject.

I lean back and raise one eyebrow. "Is that jealousy I hear in your voice?"

He frowns. "Should it be?"

I rest my chin on his chest, looking up at him. "Well, Edward is quite handsome, and charming. He seems intelligent enough. But he lacks one very specific qualification to capture my attention."

"And what is that?"

I tilt my head to the side. "He's not you."

That earns me another long, deep kiss.

It isn't long before I have to dress to sneak back to my chamber. As I tie on my cloak, Sergei approaches me from behind, kissing my neck playfully.

"When this is done, once the child is born, you should ask leave to go to the country for a while. We can have some time alone, just you and I."

"We have time alone in Oranienbaum," I say.

He kisses me again, speaking through my hair. "Not enough. I want to fall asleep with you in my arms and wake up to your face on the pillow beside me. I want the first and last thing I do every day to be kissing you."

I turn, wrapping my arms around his neck. "All right then. As soon as the baby comes."

He grins.

"And before I forget, I saw Prince Edward on my way here earlier. He was speaking with Lord Ivanovitch. They seemed to be plotting."

"What did you hear?" he asks, his face quickly falling into a stern frown.

"They said something about someone arriving tomorrow, a woman. And that it would be done by morning. I get the distinct feeling they are discussing murder."

Sergei rocks back on his heels. "Maria Theresa," he mutters. "They plan to kill the Queen of Austria."

I am shocked by his words. "No, certainly not. England is an ally to the queen. Why would they kill her?"

Sergei moves away from me, toward the window. "They have been slowly turning from Austria for the last few months, sending fewer and fewer troops, and the ones they do send are young, inexperienced soldiers. I suspect they are tired of having to fight battles on two fronts—you know they are embroiled in conflict in their new colonies as well."

I nod. "But regicide? What do they hope to gain by that?"

He doesn't have to answer. As soon as I speak the words, the full scope of their plan begins to bloom in my mind.

If she is killed here, during a peace summit, it will look as if Russia, always the puppet of Prussia, did the deed. War between Prussia and Russia would be avoided, leaving the whole of Austria at the mercy of its 'ally' England. Then England will ride in, cut off whatever it wants, and leave the rest to Prussia. The plan is genius, really. Brutally, heartlessly, genius.

"You must tell the empress," I say, and he nods.

"Yes, of course. Unless..." He trails off.

"Unless what?" I demand.

He swings his eyes to me. "If this treaty with Austria goes through, King Fredrick could retaliate, both here in Russia and on your family back in Germany."

I take a deep breath as the weight of his words settles over me. "Are you suggesting we do nothing? That we sacrifice her life to secure our own well-being?"

He reaches out, taking my hands. "You are a princess, soon to be a queen. You must understand that things are not always as simple as we would like them to be. Every choice you make from this day forward will cost lives. Whether those lives be theirs or ours rests on your shoulders."

I lick my lips. "What would you have me do?"

"I would have you think of yourself, of your own security, and that of our child above all else," he answers flatly. "In all the world, the only thing that matters to me is you. Not the conflicts, wars, or political theater of court. Only you."

He kisses me gently, and then pulls back, stroking my hair as he continues. "You are my soul and my salvation. The air that I breathe and the blood in my veins. There is nothing for me, save you. So yes, it may seem cruel, but know that I will always choose you. No matter the consequences."

In my chest, my heart picks up rhythm. Not because I doubt his words—just the opposite. But I dread when that same choice is leveled on my shoulders, because when the day comes that I must choose between my heart and my country, I honestly do not know what my choice will be.

"And what would that make me? If I knowingly let them kill her? Surely, I will be as complicit as they, in the eyes of God." I look down, and then glance up at him again. "And what kind of man could love such a person as that?"

He shakes his head and pulls me into a tight embrace. After a moment of silence, he kisses the top of my head. "I will do whatever you think best," he says finally.

I step back, lifting my hood over my hair. "Then go now and tell the empress. I would not see our nation become such a pawn, nor would I see an innocent woman die for political gain."

He sighs. "You have a good heart, Sophie."

Something in his tone makes me pause. "That didn't sound like a compliment," I say lightly.

"It wasn't," he mumbles.

Chapter

SEVEN

I slip back into my chamber quietly. Peter is still sleeping soundly, and the sun has yet to crest over the horizon, so I remove my cloak and slip into bed beside him. He stirs, rolling over to drape an arm across my torso, something that he has never, ever done before. Unsure what else to do, I let him hold me until I fall into a light, restless slumber of my own.

We are both still deeply asleep when the maids rush in. I rub my eyes and sit up, Peter's arm falling away.

"What is it?" I ask with a yawn.

"The empress is coming," Maria says hurriedly. I let her draw me from bed and lead me to the dressing area. She quickly brushes out my hair, helps me into a simple, lavender gown, and laces my shoes. Across the room, I hear Peter's valets trying to rouse him, one finally resorting to splashing water in his face. Reluctantly and with great fanfare, Peter stands, allowing the maids to busily go about straightening the bed as he dresses in the other room.

When the empress arrives, I am already sitting in the foyer, waiting for her with a pot of hot tea. She enters, and I curtsy. "Your Majesty," I say reverently.

She flicks her hand in my direction. "Where is Peter?"

He strides through the doorway shakily, as if the dim morning light is blinding to him, and takes a seat beside me.

She rolls her eyes. "I have distressing news," she begins. I fully expect her to announce that Prince Edward has been taken to the cells, or that they have cancelled the Austrian queen's visit, but neither of those things escape her lips.

"Sophia, I am sorry to say your father passed away quite suddenly two nights ago. We only just received word." She holds out a letter. "From Johanna," she adds, slipping the parchment into my hand. I take it, as if in a trance.

For a moment, I've gone numb, a loud buzzing in my ears. Then all at once the air rushes from the room and I double over, gasping for air as pain tears through me. Peter is beside me in a heartbeat, his arms around me, holding me to him.

"How dare you bring her this news now? When her health is so fragile?" He spits the words like cobra venom and tightens his hold on me, as if he could hold me tightly enough to make the tremors wracking my body stop.

Though I haven't spoken to my father since my

conversion to the Orthodox Church —an event that he strongly opposed—I always imagined he was proud of me, at least. I'd sent letters, of course, but he never responded. I always supposed he would, someday, want to reconcile. But now we never would, and I didn't even get to say goodbye. I picture him now, sitting under the apple tree behind our house, reading to my little sister as he used to read to me, while Mother looks on and my sweet brother draws shapes in the soil with a stick.

That he is gone from the world seems so wrong.

"My family," I gasp. "What will happen to them now?"

The empress' response is cold and shallow, as if she couldn't care less. "Your mother will rule over your father's lands until your brother comes of age. Either that or King Fredrick will seize the lands and declare himself protectorate over it until the boy is old enough."

My pain is quickly replaced by a flood of cold realization. Is this my punishment? Did Fredrick have my father killed because I failed to secure the treaty with Russia? Around me, the room spins and I feel like I might retch.

"How did he die?" I ask weakly, terrified to have my suspicions confirmed.

"I suggest you read the letter from your mother," she says, turning on her heel to exit. Then she adds over her shoulder, "I'm sorry for your loss."

At her words, I feel something inside me splinter and break. I struggle to my feet, shaking Peter off and moving forward, grabbing Elizabeth by the arm. "Why did you turn against Fredrick? Truly? Have I disappointed you in some way, angered you? Tell me and I will see it amended," I demand boldly.

Her face softens, and she lays a hand across my still-flat stomach. "You need only see this child safely into the world. That is the entire purpose of you now." She stares at me, her piercing blue eyes like ice on the river.

"If you think that my only value is that of a brood mare, you greatly underestimate me," I say, challenge in my voice.

She puckers her lips, turns her back on me decisively, and walks away.

All the pain in me begins to boil away in a torrent of anger. I feel my fist close around my mother's letter. Behind me, Peter touches my arm.

"You must keep calm, for the sake of the child," he warns me. "Besides, you cannot be overmuch saddened. You hadn't seen him in nearly a year. He didn't even come to the wedding."

I feel a lump like a hot coal form in my throat, and I have to take a deep, calming breath before I can turn to face him. "You are right, of course. I only need some time in quiet and prayer. I am going to go to the cathedral, to pray for him. Would you care to join me?" I offer, knowing what his response will be.

Peter detests the chapel, and he hates being in quiet solitude even more.

"I think I should see to things here." He turns to Grigori, who stands by the door, stone-faced. "Please see the duchess to the cathedral."

He nods, motioning for me to lead the way, and then falls into step behind me.

"Did you sleep at all?" I ask when we are finally out of doors and crossing the road to the massive cathedral only a stone's throw from the palace grounds.

"I did, Your Grace. I had Anton guard your door last evening, since you weren't in your room anyway."

His words pull me to a stop. "What?" I ask, sure I'd misheard him.

"I heard you leave through the servant's entrance. I followed you, discreetly, until you were safely to your destination, and then retired to my own room."

I turn to face him. There is no accusation in his voice, just simple, bold truth. "And with whom have you shared this information?" I ask.

He shakes his head. "No one, Your Grace. I would never divulge your private matters to anyone."

I exhale feeling the tension slip from my shoulders at the sincerity in his words. "And do you think less of me? Now that you see I am a flawed, imperfect creature?"

He looks at me, directly and in the eye for the first time since he made his pledge. "There is nothing on earth or in heaven that could tarnish my opinion of you, Your Grace. Nothing at all."

I blush, feeling very unworthy of such praise. "Thank you for that," I say genuinely before turning back to the cathedral.

Inside the massive structure is a chamber as breathtaking and gilded as any palace. The high ceilings are painted in works of riotous color and splendor. The white stone pillars are inlaid with gold and silver. The floor under my feet is a mosaic of beautiful, colored stones forming a depiction of the holy seal. Rows of pews line each side, a blood-red carpet stretching up to the altar like a river of crimson. At the altar, priests hum and chant while thick plumes of frankincense fill the air.

I take a seat, lowering my head to pray.

Though I haven't been in this sanctuary since my wedding day, it still fills me with awe. As I close my eyes, I feel soiled, unworthy to even seek comfort in this place. My thoughts drift. I don't want to believe that my father died at the command of King Fredrick. But, as Sergei pointed out, rulers live by a different code. For the empress or Prince Edward, murder isn't a sin—it's a necessity for survival. They must be willing to do whatever it takes to achieve their ambitions, for the good of their nations. An enemy left breathing was nothing less than a constant threat to one's own safety. Any perceived weakness attracted war like honey attracts insects.

I wonder if Sergei has told the empress about the

plot against Maria Theresa. Perhaps he was right. It would be in my best interests to see the Russo-Prussian alliance succeed. It would be in the best interests of the nation. So why was the empress so set against it? The only thing I can think is that she has information that I do not, information she has not shared with Sergei—for he would surely share any such thing with me.

Bestuzhev, I realize, lifting my chin. He would know what has turned her ear toward Austria.

Looking down at my hand, I realize I am still holding my mother's letter. I open the already broken seal and begin to read.

Empress,

I regret to tell you that my dear husband has passed away suddenly. Whether fever or a heart ailment, we do not know. With him gone, we have had to seek recompense from King Frederick for the debts owed against our properties. He assures us he will do what he can, but if you would see fit to send us a small stipend from Catherine's monthly allowance, it would greatly help our situation. Since I have not yet had the time to write to her of these tragic events, please pass the information along to her, with my love and sympathy.

We are like sisters now, through the marriage of our children, and I do hope to be invited to court soon. I would love to see you once again.

Sincerely,

Princess Johanna Von-Holstein Gorp

I ball up the letter in my hand. It is so typical of my mother, to write begging for money after the significant amount I already send her. I stand, going to the rear of the cathedral and lighting a candle for my father. I whisper a short prayer and make my way to the door. As I pass the small fireplace that heats the cold room, I toss the paper in, not even bothering to watch it burn.

When I'm outside, the bright light of day helps me clear my thoughts. I make my way back to the palace, and to the one person who might be able to help me shed some light on this madness.

The man who tried to kill me.

Chapter
EIGHT

Chancellor Bestuzhev is in the empress' private study, looking over some papers, when I arrive. He stands and bows when I enter the room. I motion for my guard to wait at the door, and he obeys without a word.

"Princess Catherine, I'm afraid the empress isn't here right now."

I nod. "I know. I came to speak with you."

He looks so surprised you'd think I just slapped him with something.

"What can I do for you?" he asks finally.

I waste no time. "I want to know what changed her mind about the treaty," I say plainly.

He blinks rapidly. "I'm sure I don't know what you mean."

I hold up my hand. "I know you didn't want me here, badly enough that you thought to have me killed. Surely, by now, you know that was a mistake."

He lowers his eyes, his expression souring.

I continue. "Yet, even for that, I forgave you. Not

only that, I saved you after Peter's attack. I know that we will never be friends, but I believe you owe me."

"What, pray tell, do I owe you?"

I straighten. "An explanation."

He ponders the idea for a minute before taking a seat at the desk. "Very well. I suppose I can offer you that."

I fold my arms and wait for him to begin.

"It was your mother," he says, and I feel my face fall.

"What?"

He nods. "While she was here, we intercepted many letters between her and King Fredrick. Most of them were of no importance, commentary on the food and music—benign things. Then we intercepted a message of another kind, one that insinuated she and Count Lestocq were plotting with Fredrick to liberate young Ivan from prison and steal him away to Prussia."

I suck in a sharp breath.

Empress Elizabeth had usurped the throne from her sister's grandnephew Ivan, who was only an infant when Empress Anna died, leaving the kingdom to him. To see Ivan on the throne would have meant that Elizabeth, Peter the First's legitimized daughter, would be passed over for the crown—something she was not about to allow to happen. Though the coup was a success and no lives were lost, she had sent the baby into prison, where he had been rotting away ever since.

Rumors swirl around the boy. Some say he's gone mad, growing up in such conditions. Others say that in her mercy, the empress had handed him off to a peasant family to raise as their own, with no knowledge of his true lineage. Whatever his fate, those who opposed Elizabeth's reign would love to get their hands on him, to use him to divide the country and incite civil war in Russia.

"It was a clear and bold move against the empress and her reign. How could she trust Fredrick after such treachery? She reached out to Maria Theresa not long after having your mother removed from court."

I swallow hard as the final pieces fall into place. There is small comfort for me in knowing it was not I who soured the empress on the treaty, but my faithless, selfish, idiotic mother. If my father did indeed die as retribution, his blood is on her hands and not my own.

Out the corner of my eye, I see a small, lead stamp, next to the larger, gold one which I know carries the empress' royal seal. It sits on a shelf near the far wall. I step between it and Bestuzhev, closing the distance between us.

"Thank you for your honesty," I say, my voice barely above a whisper. "Please know that I have forgiven you for your actions. Whether you sought that forgiveness or not, it is yours all the same."

He lowers his chin. "I am not proud of what I've done, but it was for what I believed to be the good of the empire. Still, you are kinder than I deserve."

"Sometimes, we must make difficult choices. I see that very clearly now," I say finally.

He nods, and I take my leave. Grigori falls into step behind me as I move down the hallway.

"You look pale, Your Grace. Is everything well?" he asks.

I frown. "No. I have the information I've been seeking, and it wasn't at all what I expected."

"What can I do?" he asks.

I turn to him. "Fetch Sergei, tell him it is urgent, and have him meet me in the library. Then, find me the fastest horseman in the garrison and bring him to the library as well."

He bows and hurries off as I make my way to the library, a plan forming in my mind with each step.

Perhaps there is a way to salvage the situation after all.

❧

When Sergei arrives, I'm already writing my first letter.

He rushes into the room breathlessly, as if he's been running. "What is it?" he asks, looking me over. "Are you all right?"

I look up from my parchment. "I have a plan," I say flatly.

He expels a long breath. "Your guard said it was

urgent. I was afraid there was a problem."

I look down, continuing my letter. "There is a problem. Have you not received the news? My father is dead."

In silence, he pulls out the chair beside me and takes a seat. "I'm so sorry."

I shrug it off, not willing to think of that now. "My mother was plotting with Fredrick to depose Elizabeth and put Ivan on the throne," I blurt out, not looking up to see his expression.

"Are you certain?" he asks with a tone of surprise.

"I am."

"So what are you planning to do?"

I pause, setting down the quill and blowing the wet ink. "I'm drafting a letter to Maria Theresa, warning her of the plot against her life." I slide the paper across the table so he can read it. "I assume you haven't yet spoken with the empress about what I overheard?"

He shakes his head, his dark hair falling across his brow and into his eyes. "No, she's been occupied all day. I haven't been able to get an audience, which is especially odd. I just assumed Bestuzhev was keeping her from my influence, lest I change her mind about the treaty."

Pushing his hair back, he reads over my letter. "An anonymous warning. Excellent idea. But it says that the empress is aware of the plot and brings her here anyway. You make it sound as if she is a co-conspirator."

I nod, gently biting my lower lip. "You are right on one matter—we cannot allow the treaty with Austria to proceed. It could be disastrous for not just my remaining family in Prussia, but for the entire nation. Austria is not strong enough to stand against us—they wouldn't dare. But Fredrick is looking for any excuse to topple Elizabeth and put someone of his choosing on the throne, and he will carve himself off a healthy chunk of the country in the process."

"That is very clever. But should they communicate, the ruse will be discovered," he points out.

"Yes. Which is why I am writing another letter, from an anonymous member of Maria Theresa's company. This one will explain that Maria Theresa has reconsidered the offer of a treaty with Russia because they have uncovered a plot against the queen and believe Elizabeth to be a participant. By the time the two have cooled their tempers enough to speak to each other, the damage will have been done, the trust broken. If Elizabeth maintains ignorance to the plot, she looks like a weak fool who cannot control her own court. If she admits to it, she salvages her relationship with Prussia, and they can share the spoils when the queen is defeated. I must rely on you to clarify that situation to her, though you must lead her to the conclusion so she believes the thought to be her own."

When I look up at him again, he's grinning wildly. "Look at you, Little Snow Queen. How very far you've come in such a short time. Someday, you will be a force to be reckoned with," he says thoughtfully.

I take the letter back and fold it carefully. Taking the small, lead seal I'd stolen only minutes before from my sleeve, I seal it with bright red wax. When I finish, it is the rough image of an eagle inlaid over a cross, Bestuzhev's personal seal, on the letter.

"I fear I already am," I respond, unable to gather any emotion at all about my actions. There is no warmth or guilt, just cold, empty practicality.

Just then, Grigori and another man enter the room and bow. I stand and wave them over.

"Your Grace," Grigori begins. "This is Lieutenant Rossier. Our fastest rider, as you requested."

Rossier bows, bringing his fist to his chest. "Your Grace."

I nod and hand him the letter. "Lieutenant, I need you to take the fastest horse and ride out to intercept Queen Maria Theresa's company. Find her, and only her, and give her this letter. Tell her only that it was sent from someone very close to the empress, but do not say from whom. Any message she sends in return, you bring directly to me. Can I trust you on this matter?" I ask sternly.

He nods, his eyes wide. "Of course, Your Grace."

"Good, go now. There is no time to be lost."

With that, he scurries from the room, leaving me with only Sergei and Grigori, who watch on in silence as I write my last letter, sealing it with a plain, round stone.

I hand it to Sergei, who accepts it slowly.

"You realize, with one stroke of your pen, you may well have altered the course of history," he says in hushed tones.

I nibble on my lip a bit more. "I cannot think of that now. I can only think of this day, and what must be done in it. History can be tomorrow's problem."

He smiles and stands. Leaning over, I think he's going to kiss me, and then he glances quickly to Grigori and hesitates.

"It's all right. I have no secrets from my guard."

"Is that wise?" he asks.

Reaching up, I take him by the back of the neck and pull him down until our lips are almost touching. "I trust him as I trust you. Now kiss me and go."

He does as I command.

When he's gone, I stand. I'm about to leave when a familiar volume catches my eye from the bookshelf. As if unable to stop myself, I walk over and slide it from the shelf.

It's a copy of John Wilmot's *Letters to His Mistress*, one of my favorite books of verse. I crack it open and, for just a moment, my heart races, expecting a hastily scribbled note to fall from between the pages as it had so many times before. But there is nothing, no evidence at all that it had once been used to carry secret messages to the man I loved. It is as empty as I feel.

I slide my fingers over the text slowly. Though Alexander is long gone from Russia, I still feel him here. It is worse being back in Winter Palace, where everything I see reminds me of him, where every moment I expect to hear his laugh echoing down the halls. Taking the book with me, I return to the table and my parchment. Though I know he will never read my words, it feels good to write them. It feels like I am that same girl I once was, innocent and blissful, never for a moment thinking that the darkness would creep in and steal him away from me.

Paris,

The day is long, and I weary of this place. Would that I could be born again, that I might once more touch your face. Though you are far and I am here, I miss you still, my love, my dear.

Helen

I tuck the letter into the pages, only scarcely able to hold back the ache in my heart, a wound that never seems to truly heal. Though I find solace and comfort in Sergei's arms, there is still a small, mutinous part of me that longs for what I have lost. I try to ignore it, but it is there all the same. I do not know if I will ever have the courage to love anyone so fully ever again. Perhaps that is shallow or cold, but I do not think I could survive it. Absently, my hand goes to the small satchel hanging from my neck by a thin cord. Though it's tucked away under my bodice, the feel of it under my fingers gives me strength. The pouch of German soil is a constant reminder of where I came from, and what I've sacrificed to get where I am.

Love is never rational. Alexander's voice echoes in my head, and I force it away.

Re-shelving the volume, I gather myself and leave the library, allowing whatever lingering feelings I have to remain closed in the pages of that book.

That night, there is great commotion as a flustered servant rushes into my room to announce that the dinner and ball have been canceled due to the empress being too exhausted to attend. Around me, my ladies groan and complain as we work on our stitchery while Maria plays the piano.

"Ladies, if you will excuse me, I am going to go see to the empress," I announce, standing and motioning for Maria to join me.

"But what are we going to do all night?" the youngest girl, Birdie, complains, tossing her yellow hair over her shoulder.

I pause. "Why don't you go and gather some food from the kitchens and speak to a few of the musicians? We can have a small supper and dance tonight in our chamber," I offer.

She and the others perk up at the idea.

"Oh, that would be wonderful! I will let the cooks know," she says.

"And I'll tell the grand duke and his men," another chimes in.

I wave them off to their excitement and take Maria's arm.

"Are you certain that's a good idea?" she whispers once we are in the hall.

I shake my head. "No, probably not. But Peter will be in a sour mood without some sort of entertainment, and we do need to eat. Do watch over the ladies though, and make sure they don't take the event to extremes."

"Of course," she replies.

I hear a scuffle and glance up just in time to see Peter racing toward me at a run, slowing to a halt just before knocking into me.

"Oh, pardon me. Come, Catherine. There is something I want you to see," he says, tugging gently at my arm. He's flushed and smiling his handsome, boyish grin, and I have no choice but to allow him to drag me along.

Chapter
NINE

As we race down the hall, laughing like children, I can't help but remember my first days at court. I'd been so naive. My only thoughts were of winning Peter's heart. I wanted some silly, fairy tale sort of life like I'd read about in books, a story where my prince would be handsome, kind, and love me above all others. I'd been looking for that, and when Peter fell short of that fantasy, I'd hardened myself against him and given my heart to another.

But for the moment, we are happy. I know it won't last long—it never does—but I allow myself to enjoy it while I can.

When he finally pulls me into a small room at the end of the hall, there is a group of people already there. Two of his stewards, a handful of the lords and ladies, and one of his guards. Grigori and Maria burst into the room behind us, both panting.

"What is it?" I ask.

He waves me over to the far wall where a long, colorful tapestry hangs, a depiction of the Imperial crest woven into the linen. Brushing it aside with one hand, he uses the tip of his foot to draw over a small, velvet footstool and motions for me to step up, holding his free hand out to me.

When I step up, I feel Peter's arm protectively at my back and I stare at the wall. A small flicker of light catches my eye and I press my face against it, peering through the small hole.

At first, I'm not certain what I'm seeing, then the sounds come, faint and muffled by the wall separating the rooms.

It's the empress, I realize, and she isn't alone. For a moment, all I can see is a mop of dark hair and two bodies writhing against each other, and a knot forms in my belly.

Sergei?

Then he moves, rolling her over, and I see that it's not Sergei at all, but rather a very salacious, very flushed Prince Edward.

No wonder the empress has been 'occupied' all afternoon. With an exasperated blush climbing up my face, and just as I'm about to step down, her door flies open and Sergei storms in. One of her guards tries to restrain him, but Sergei pushes his way past and into the room. If he's surprised at all by what he sees, he doesn't show it.

And the empress, for her part, looks completely unimpressed with the spectacle of his arrival even as Edward struggles to cover his more intimate parts with the heaps of blankets.

"Lord Salkov, I hope you have a reason for this disrespect," she says coolly, not bothering to cover herself as she wriggles free from the arms of her lover and sits up.

Sergei bows. "Deepest apologies, Your Majesty, but I've been trying to reach you all day. An urgent matter has come to my attention and—"

She cuts him off. "You can leave your matter with the chancellor. I am occupied." Leaning forward, she licks her lips. "Or is that the real reason you've come so boldly into my chamber? Would you care to stay and join us? It has been quite some time and you were always one of my favorite companions."

I feel my hands ball into fists when she speaks.

"That is high praise, My Empress, but not my intention."

She pouts, scooting off the bed. As she stands there, completely naked, I'm transfixed, not by her beauty, but by her boldness as she strides across the room. She places a hand on Sergei's chest, and he covers it with his own.

A rage builds inside me, a cold fury I've never experienced. It demands I barge into that room myself and remove her hand from him—consequences be damned. I'm not sure what shred of sanity keeps me still, but only moments later, I am thankful for it.

Sergei holds up my letter. "A plot has been uncovered. Someone here, in your company, has plotted against Queen Maria Theresa, and worse than that, she discovered it before we did. She has revoked her offer of treaty and is returning to Austria."

The effect on the empress is immediate, as if he's thrown a barrel of cold water on her. She snatches the parchment and reads the words for herself.

"What do you know of this?" she demands. "Who sent this letter?"

Sergei shrugs. "One of her officials to be sure. I've verified its authenticity. And as to the matter that she speaks, I think her informants are quite correct. I have discovered whispers of such a plot. I have only just taken Lord Ivanovitch into custody. He will be questioned and any information we attain will be used to severely punish those who would undermine your authority here."

She nods slowly, not looking back over her shoulder to Prince Edward, who lies, still as a mouse, tangled in her bed sheets. "Prince Edward, I think it is best if you leave us now," she says grudgingly.

He obeys quickly and without a word. Scooping up his trousers and shirt, he covers himself as best he can and scurries past Sergei without meeting his eyes.

"This will ruin everything," she whimpers loudly.

Sergei moves to her wardrobe, taking a thick, red cloak and moving to drape it over her shoulders, momentarily concealing her from my view. Then he kneels before her, taking her hands in his. "Elizabeth, Bess, I know this troubles you, and for that, I am sorry."

"How could I be so blind to the happenings of my own court?" she says, her voice high and nasal.

I raise an eyebrow. *She could start by ejecting the devious, self-serving men from her boudoir*, I think miserably.

Sergei says nothing.

"You must write to her immediately, tell her I knew nothing of this. Tell her the matter is being taken care of. She will be safe here, give her my assurance," she says.

Sergei frowns. "Bess, you realize this means she had spies inside your court? How would she have discovered the plot if not for that?" The empress looks stricken by his implication. He continues. "And to admit openly that this went on under your nose, it might make you look vulnerable, as if you are unable to control your own court. That is not a message we can afford to send, not now, with Fredrick looking for any perceived weakness in your rule."

She nods slowly. "You are right, of course." Reaching out, she cups the side of his face in her hand, and the rage builds once more inside me. Knowing they were once intimate is one matter, witnessing it is quite another. "We will have to be proactive. Write to Fredrick, tell him our plan to ferret out her spies at court has been successful. Tell him the treaty with Austria was all a ruse to make her show her hand, to get her off her seat of power and into my custody."

"Clever strategy," he says thoughtfully.

She exhales and smiles warmly, her fingers cupping his chin. "What would I do without you?"

Afraid that she is going to lean forward and kiss him—something I could not bear to witness—I step down from the stool.

"What was it? What did you see?" Peter asks excitedly.

I shake my head. "The empress has decided not to pursue the treaty with Austria," I say softly, taking his hand and leading him away from the others, who are all clamoring for a chance to look through the peephole.

"This is wonderful," Peter says cheerfully. "King Fredrick will be so relieved."

"That's not all. Peter, did you know King Fredrick conspired to remove your aunt from the throne?"

He pales at my words, his expression a mixture of shock and disbelief only for a moment before laughing out loud. "Not to worry, Little Mother. I'm sure he only sought to hasten my own rise to power. Great men like Fredrick can only abide the delicate sensibilities of women so long on the field of leadership."

I'm not sure what surprises me more, his steadfast faith in Fredrick, or his casual dismissal of the possible death of his aunt. I know I should say more, beg him to see the truth, that it was not Peter but Ivan that Fredrick thought to install, but I say nothing of it. Part of me is afraid he might lash out at me; the other isn't certain it even matters. Peter or Ivan on the throne, either way, Fredrick wins. They are both his puppets.

Behind us, the commotion grows as two men fight to get on the stool, pushing each other and laughing merrily.

Giving up on the matter, I change the subject. "This isn't right. Peter, you must put an end to this and get these people out of here. If the empress discovers what you've done..." I don't get the chance to finish that sentence.

The door swings open and Empress Elizabeth, probably still nude under her regal robes, strides into the room, Sergei at her heels.

Chapter
Ten

"T hat is the meaning of this?" she demands.

To say we are all stunned into silence would be an understatement. We are frozen, caught in the most cardinal of sins. Behind us, the rest of the group falls to their knees. Only Peter and I stand tall, mouths agape, at her imposing figure.

"Well? Explain yourselves!" she demands once more, her voice like a clap of thunder.

I open my mouth, but it is Peter who speaks first. "Aunt, the maids only discovered this today, while cleaning. They thought to tell you, but you were occupied, so they brought the matter to me. I came in to investigate the situation," he lies smoothly.

I have never seen the empress turn such a brilliant shade of red. Stepping forward, she reaches out and slaps Peter with all her might. She begins a tirade upon him so full of vile curses that my ears cannot make sense of it all.

"And you thought to bring in an audience?" she spits finally. "I am ordained by God, anointed with holy oil. I am a vessel for his will and a holy object in every way. Only the worthy may look upon me. And you have violated my sanctity."

Just when I think Peter has been thoroughly shamed, I see him look up, a wicked glimmer in his eye.

"I just assumed there wasn't a male left in the palace that hadn't already seen you naked, so what was the harm?"

She slaps him again, this time hard enough that blood trickles from the side of his mouth. But there is no fear in him, only defiance. I rush to his side, feigning concern, but really hoping only to prevent her from attacking him again. I'm afraid of what he might do to her if she strikes him once more.

"Peter," I mutter, taking his face in my hands. He looks down at me and his expression cools, a pleased grin taking root.

"I'm fine, Little Mother. Don't fret over me."

I nod, as if relieved, and turn to the empress, still standing between them. "Our deepest apologies, Your Majesty. We meant no disrespect, truly," I say.

She scoffs. "Oh, I know. I heard you urging my idiot nephew to abandon this folly only moments before I entered the room." The words should be a compliment to my character, but somehow, they come out bitter and angry. "Aren't you just perfect? Saintly, angelic Catherine, the epitome of goodness and virtue."

My eyes widen. Whatever I have done, the empress hates me now. I can hear it in her words and see it when she looks at me. I just don't understand why. I've done everything she asked for, toed every line. Yet, somehow, I have fallen from her favor, and I do not know what to do to fix it.

I look down, not wanting to challenge her by meeting her eyes. "I am sorry to have displeased you so, Your Majesty."

She scoffs at me again and moves past us, to the group cowering in our wake. "The rest of you, follow me. I will teach you a lesson about spying on the Empress of Russia."

They slink after her like beaten dogs. Only when she is gone do I allow myself to take a full breath. Sergei passes me a look I cannot read and I turn my attention back to Peter, gently wiping the blood from his chin with the sleeve of my gown.

"You'll ruin your dress," he says gently.

I smirk. "I don't care, as long as you are all right."

In a move that takes me by surprise, he takes my hands in his, lowering his chin so his blue eyes are level with my own.

"Do you love me?" he asks.

It's so sudden and unexpected that I hesitate. Do I love Peter? He is my husband in the eyes of man and God. Though I was forced into my infidelity as a matter of survival, I have found love there, with Sergei.

My hesitation is enough to make him balk. He drops my hands forcefully and steps back.

"You frighten me, sometimes," I say honestly. "I want to love you, truly more than anything, I want to love you. I am trying."

He shakes his head. "Love isn't that hard. You either love someone or you don't. You shouldn't have to try."

"Do you love me?" I whisper as he walks past me to leave.

He looks over his shoulder. "I have loved you since the first time I saw your face, when we were nine years old. I loved you then, and I love you now. Though I think I hate you sometimes too, and just as deeply."

Then, with nothing else, he leaves me alone to replay his words in my head.

When evening finally comes, I'm exhausted and ready to put my head to rest. I've all but forgotten about my promise of entertainment in my chambers. Not wanting to disappoint my ladies, I push through. We dress in our smallest panniers, not wanting to overtake the modest room with our excessive gowns, and don colorful masks one of the girls has ferreted from the empress' private stash of costumes. Mine resembles a set of butterfly wings, in scrolled, black satin, matching my dark silk and lace gown. Peter, never one to miss a party, comes in a pale white mask with a long, pointed nose. Though I'm not certain who all is in attendance, it seems as if half the palace is crammed into my small apartments, dancing, drinking, and eating merrily.

As I dance, a familiar hand takes mine, pulling me to the corner of the room. I don't have to ask him to remove his mask to know it's my Sergei. His piercing, ocean-wave eyes give him away.

"I wanted to speak to you about earlier," he says, his voice too low for anyone but me to hear over the loud violins.

I feel myself frown. The image of Elizabeth, her hands on him, is seared into my mind like a terrible burn. I know I will never be rid of it, and it hurts in ways I don't expect.

"You don't need to explain anything to me," I begin. "I knew what your relationship with the empress was before I gave myself to you. You never made a secret of it."

Then I pause, taking a drink of water. "Though, perhaps seeing it was a bit… unsettling," I admit.

He grins.

"Oh, does my displeasure amuse you?" I counter harshly.

"No, of course not, I was only thinking." He takes a beat. "I'm glad you were jealous."

I make a face. "I never said I was jealous."

He smirks again. "You didn't have to."

I move to walk away, and he catches my arm.

"Wait. I only meant that it makes me happy because, to be frank, I was afraid you wouldn't care at all."

"I shouldn't," I say, more to myself than him.

"But you do. It bothers you because you love me, though you have never said as much. I had begun to wonder what I meant to you, and now I know," he finishes.

Glancing up, I see that Peter has halted his dance and is watching us intently. I incline my head to Sergei. "This conversation will have to conclude at another time. Peter is watching and I should go to him," I say.

Sergei bows and wanders off in one direction while I go the other, making a beeline for Peter. When I am close enough, I lean into him. "Sergei says the empress' temper is cooling. Hopefully, her rage will only last as long as her infatuations seem to."

Peter smiles, taking my hand, and together, we dance until the sun is rising and its light begins to shine through the windows.

Though most everyone has left, a few remain. Some sleeping on the couches, others passed out in corners or chairs. When I can take no more, I extricate myself from Peter's grasp. "I am too tired," I say weakly. "I must get to bed."

He looks as if he's about to protest, so I put my hand on my belly protectively. Seeing the gesture, his expression changes to one of concern.

"Yes, yes, of course, Little Mother. What was I thinking? Here, let me tuck you in," he offers, leading me through the next set of doors and into our private chamber.

"Are any of my ladies still standing?" I ask with a light laugh as I slip out of my shoes and begin trying to escape my gown.

He chuckles too. "I doubt it. Here, allow me."

At my back, he quickly and skillfully begins to unlace my bodice, slipping it off my shoulders till it falls to the floor. My panniers come off next, though he lifts them over my head before tossing them aside. It's not until that moment that I realize my position. Standing there in my undergarments, I might as well be naked. While I've dressed and undressed in his presence many times, it was never like this. Never had he touched me in this way. I stiffen as I feel his fingers loosening the laces of my corset, relaxing it until I can take a deep breath and then it, too, falls to the ground, and only my sheer shift remains, separating his skin from mine.

Panic sets in. What do I do now? Should I go to him, embrace him as a wife should her husband? Would he even have me? The idea terrifies me. I can't help thinking back to our wedding night, to his hands choking the life from me as he called me vile names, his threats and his promise to kill me if he had to.

But what if this is my chance? An opportunity to

change my sad fate? Could we be happy? Was that even a possibility? And if so, what would that mean for Sergei? My heart aches at the thought.

Would I have to give him up?

Time itself seems to slow as I feel Peter lower his head, pressing a kiss to my neck, just behind my ear, then another to my shoulder as he gently slips the shift to the side so it falls just a little. His lips burn like a fever—a mad, strange, tingling warmth. I want to pull away, I realize, but it's too late for that now.

I turn slowly, my eyes on the floor as I move. Then, once I'm facing him, I very slowly raise my eyes until they meet his.

There is a hunger in his face that I do not expect. He glances down, his eyes fixated on the rise and fall of my chest.

"What's this?" he asks curiously, reaching out and taking hold of the small, brown satchel resting between my breasts.

I swallow hard, following his gaze. "It's a pouch of German soil. It was a gift," I add absently.

I feel his fingers tighten around it.

"Thoughtful. Who gave it to you?" he asks, his tone dangerous.

Opening my mouth, I fully intend to lie, but he is glaring at me, and the words freeze in my throat. I gasp, unable to stop myself, and realization blossoms in his face.

"Who. Gave. It. To. You?" he demands again,

tugging at the cord so it digs into the back of my neck.

"Alexander." The truth rushes from me like a whirlwind and Peter reddens, fighting to restrain his anger. He pulls harder and the cord snaps, leaving the pouch in his fist.

"And you wear it still? All this time?" he asks. Though he already knows the answer, somehow hearing me say the words will make it real in his mind. "I give you jewels and yet you wear this?"

"Yes, but it's not why you think," I say quickly, reaching out to him.

He smacks my hand away. "And what do I think?"

I lick my lips. "I wear it to remind me of how far I've come, of what I've left behind to be here, with you." His expression doesn't change, so I add, "And our baby."

It's a sad card to play, but at the moment, it is all I have and all that might stem his temper.

He holds his hand out to me. "Then take it. Take it, go down to the riverbank, and toss it away. If you have left those things behind, then leave them all behind."

There is challenge in his voice, and I dare not allow my sadness to show.

"Of course, as you wish. First thing tomorrow morning. We can go together, you and I, and toss it away."

"It is morning," he corrects me. "So go now, and be done with it."

I look down at myself. "You want me to go out like this?"

With a low grumble, he grabs my thick, white cloak from the hanger. "Here." He tosses it at me, and I catch it.

I put it on quickly, fastening it around my neck. "Thank you," I say feebly, trying to think of some way to salvage the delicate peace we have only just achieved. "For allowing me to do this, to prove that my loyalty is, and always will be, to you."

He sits on the edge of the bed and nods. "Go now."

I scurry out the door, through the main chamber, and into the hall. Even my guard, whoever Grigori sent to watch me for the evening, is asleep at his post. I wonder for a moment if I should wake him, but I decide better of it. It's only a short walk to the river and the sun is nearly full up.

With bare feet, I practically run down the stairs, out the side door, and into the woods. Thankfully, it is finally warming, and the snow is all but gone as I make my way to the river bridge. Once I'm there, I look down at the small pouch in my hand and for some reason, it feels as if my heart has caved in. I don't want to throw it away. It has been my touchstone for far too long. But Peter knows where it came from and if he ever catches sight of it again, it will serve as a reminder that he has been doubly betrayed. Once by Alexander, and once by only the mere memory of him.

Mustering my resolve, I draw back and launch

it into the water, and then I turn back to the palace, barely visible through the trees. My heart aches, as if I've thrown a piece of myself away as well.

It takes me longer to get back. I am bone weary now, and I hope Peter has long since fallen asleep. Though most of the household staff is awake, they remain in the kitchens for now, probably trying to keep from waking the empress before her time. I climb the red-carpeted staircase and turn toward my chambers.

I never see who comes up behind me. I only feel hands on my back and then, before I can move to defend myself, I begin to fall.

Chapter
ELEVEN

I can barely think through the pain. I open my eyes and it feels as if every bone in my body is broken. I lay at the bottom of the grand staircase, unable to move, unable to even scream for help. But someone must have heard the commotion because one of the kitchen women rushes to my side, screaming.

"Help! Help! Fetch the doctor! Help!"

And I lie there, praying for death to take me swiftly.

For what feels like a very long time, it seems that it has. I cannot see, for I cannot open my eyes. The pain is mostly gone, only a thick, deep ache filling me with each breath. There are voices, Peter, Sergei, Maria, even the empress. A hand strokes my hair, touches my cheek. I cannot respond to it. My body no longer obeys me.

The next time I open my eyes, it's because I feel a strange weight on me. I blink and the light is dim, the flicker of candles casting shadows in my bedroom. Looking down, I see that Peter lies beside me, his head resting across my belly. With great effort, I raise my hand and gently stroke his golden hair. He shakes. It takes me some time to realize he's crying.

I fall to sleep once more.

Though I have no sense of how much time passes, I imagine it must be a great deal. There are more voices, more sensations of being touched, damp rags placed across my head.

"Can you hear me?" a voice asks.

I answer without opening my eyes. "I hear you."

"Thank God," comes the reply. "Fetch the grand duke."

It's the empress. I know the tone from the last time she tended to me so kindly.

"There, there," she coos, wiping my face.

I fight until my eyes peel open. "What? What happened?"

Wringing out the rag in a basin of water, she replaces it on my head. "You fell down the stairs," she says matter-of-factly.

I remember, vaguely, but the memory grows stronger. "Pushed," I say quickly. "I was pushed."

She pauses only for the briefest moment. "Are you certain?"

I nod, and it sends the room spinning.

"The doctor says you hit your head badly, but you will recover." Her voice is sad, almost cold.

I'm about to let the darkness take me again when a thought snaps into my brain. I reach out and grab her arm to steady myself. "What about the baby?" I ask.

She frowns, wringing her hands. "The baby is gone," she whispers.

I feel something inside me shatter like glass. Gone. Just like that. I never even got to hold him. Why? Why would God punish me like this? Was it my sin that stole my child from me? The tears come freely but quietly and I roll to my side, looking away so she won't see them. I clutch my middle, as if I could somehow make it all a bad dream, and not a painful reality.

I hear Peter enter the room, though I don't look at him. I feel the empress stand, leaving the bed, and I feel Peter sit in her place.

"I'm so sorry," I manage through the tears. I'm shaking now, my whole body racked with tremors that threaten to collapse me from the inside.

I expect wrath, rage. I have cost Peter the one thing he wanted more than anything else in the world. I expect bitter accusations, and I steel myself for them. But the words do not come.

I feel Peter lay down beside me, then, unexpectedly, he takes me in his arms and caresses me. "I'm so sorry. I never should have sent you to the river. It was careless and stupid and now, we have lost everything." He pauses. "Can you forgive me?"

I stumble over my words, so I just nod and his arms tighten around me.

Somewhere, I realize, Sergei is grieving the loss of his child as well. Only he must do it alone, in secret.

The realization breaks my heart a little more, making it hard to breathe.

What a terrible, shameful mess I have made of things.

I let Peter hold me until I fall into a shallow, restless sleep.

It's days before I'm well again. I've lost weeks to the trauma, and I can't bring myself to stay in bed another minute. With the help of my ladies, I bathe, dress, and brush out my hair.

I can hear the feast below. Elizabeth, never one to let others' grief sour her merriment, is hosting an Italian Opera, and I am desperate for a change of scenery.

My dress is soft white organza, and it flows loosely at my waist. I'm far too bruised in my ribs to attempt a corset, and it still pains me to breathe from time to time. When I arrive, flanked by my ladies, the room grows still. I take my seat beside Peter, who sits, as he used to, with Elizavetta at his right hand. She is thinner than I remember, with shadows under her eyes that make her look weary.

The moment I see her, I know—it was she who pushed me. She glances up at me, a mixture of surprise and rage etched into the line of her mouth.

It's all I have not to lunge for her, scratching her

eyes from her head in front of the entire court.

Peter stands, pulling out my chair for me. I sit slowly and with great effort.

The empress stands, making a toast. "To Grand Duchess Catherine, we are glad you are well and able to join us once more," she says. The others join in and salute me with their glasses.

When she finishes, I stand, lifting my chin high into the air. "I have an announcement of my own. This loss is a tragedy, not only for the House of Romanov, but also for all of Russia. Our heir was not lost in an accident. He was taken from you in an act of violence. I want to assure you all that we will discover the persons behind this heinous act of treachery, and that person will be dealt with swiftly and decisively. I ask only that you all, my dear friends and Lords of the Empire, keep us in your prayers, that God may see fit to bless you with another heir very soon."

There is a moment of stunned silence, and then, as my words sink in, a sense of bold outrage fills the room, growing feverish. Glasses are lifted, cheers are sent up, and blessings offered. But mostly, there is a sense of rage about them. I have not made this my loss, but theirs, and I know that any of them who know anything will be only too eager to come forth with the information. I sit back down, and the empress glares at me over her glass of wine.

Beside me, Peter leans in. "What are you doing?" he demands.

I lower my chin. "I know you feel responsible for our loss, but you needn't. I did not fall down those stairs, Peter. I was pushed. I remember it very clearly."

"By whom?" he asks, his voice louder than the empress would like, judging by the glare she levels in his direction.

I take a drink of wine and it is bitter on my tongue. "I did not see the person responsible, though I have my suspicions," I say loud enough for Elizavetta to hear. "But I assure you, I will find out."

"And when you do, I will skin him alive," Peter says with just a bit too much enthusiasm.

"In the meantime, you two should see to the production of a new heir, immediately," the empress says as she takes a sip of wine.

Unsure what to say to that, I look to Peter, but he is distracted by something Elizavetta is saying in his ear, and it makes him laugh. I scan the crowd, and my eyes lock on Sergei's. He's not far from me, talking with some of the lords with a fervent expression.

I stand. "I'm sorry; I need a moment of air."

"I'll join you," Peter offers.

I stop him with a quick kiss on his cheek. It surprises him almost as much as it surprises me. "No, dear. You stay, enjoy your company. I will only be a moment," I say.

I walk out of the banquet hall and out onto the terrace. It isn't long before Sergei joins me. He stands close, his front pressed to my back, and he strokes my arm gently.

"Are you all right?" he asks.

I hear my voice crack when I speak. "No, I don't think I am. I feel so lost. And all I want to do is throw myself into your arms, but I can't. We must be careful, so very careful."

He hushes me, kissing the top of my head. "This was the second time I thought I'd lost you," he whispers.

I step forward, out of his grasp. "When I woke up, and they told me the baby was gone, I honestly thought Peter might kill me. But then, all I could think of was you, and how alone and sad you must be," I admit. "Even now, knowing that you suffered that loss alone, it breaks my heart."

"You are well, and that is enough to soothe any injury," he says earnestly.

I take a deep breath. "The empress is right. We must try for an heir again as soon as possible," I say slowly, trying to let the words sink in. "I tricked Peter once before, but I do not think it will work this time. And the idea of being with him…" I don't know how to continue, so I let the rest of the words fall away.

"I hate the thought of him touching you," Sergei says, his voice almost a growl.

His words make me feel better and worse all at the same time.

I steady myself, grasping the metal railing of the balcony. "Whatever happens now, know that I love you, Sergei. Truly and always. And know that as soon as I'm able, I will find my way back to you."

I don't dare meet his eyes as I turn and slip past him, rejoining the feast at Peter's side. When we stand to head to the theater for the opera, he holds out his arm to me, a gesture that only serves to make Elizavetta look even more miserable.

I will have words with that treacherous slattern later. For now, I bask in Peter's attentions, inwardly relishing her torment.

We take our seats in the lavish theater. With intricate gold parquetry from floor to ceiling, the oval room is one of the most elaborate in the palace, despite its rather small size. With six rows of velvet-covered chairs lined up at the base of the stage, and three half-moon benches behind those, the theater only seats about thirty people in all. Close quarters, to be sure. However, the chairs are reserved for the royal family and their personal favorites only. The empress takes her seat in the center of the first row, flanked by Bestuzhev and Sergei. Peter and I slip into the row directly behind, and he sits directly at her back, which places me behind Sergei. I half expect him to motion for Elizavetta to take his other side, but it is Mikhail who receives the nod, leaving the pouting redhead to take a seat with the ladies and nobles in the benches.

The stewards snuff the candles and douse the lamps, and the opera begins.

"I have missed your company," I whisper to Peter

as softly as possible, taking his hand in mine.

He brings it to his lips and kisses it quickly. "As have I. Are you well enough to ride with me tomorrow?"

"I would love to," I say honestly. Riding is one of my purest joys, and one of the few activities in which Peter can match me. "Would you come to my room later? Perhaps we could share some wine, and you could tell me all that I've missed in my convalescence?"

Since I've been recovering, Peter has been moved into his own apartment, and while part of me is overjoyed to have my own space again, that kind of separation won't sit well with the empress for long, not now.

"I will consider it," he says finally.

I'm surprised at the disappointment I feel.

The opera continues and eventually Peter drifts off, his head rolling to the side in his sleep. I sigh heavily. Peter has never been one for theater, or any of the subtle, artistic pursuits of life. He finds them dull and pointless, almost as dull as I find his constant military drills and his desire to act out old battles with wooden soldiers on his map table. We are, at our cores, two very different creatures. *Never has such a poor match been made*, I think miserably.

When the lights are finally lit, Mikhail nudges Peter gently, rousing him from his slumber. He walks me back to my room in virtual silence, his men and my ladies following us. Behind us, they talk of the weather, the newest fashions from Paris, even the scandalous Madame de Pompadour.

"They say she has the beauty of an angel, that no woman alive could be her rival," one of the ladies says with a deep, longing sigh. "They say that King Louis fell at his feet before her."

"Then he is no king at all, to let a pretty face render him so low," Peter scoffs. "Besides, if one is looking for the most beautiful woman in Europe, one needs look no further than Russia."

Several of them mutter in agreement, but I can't help wonder if it is me he speaks of, or another. I dare not ask.

We are nearly to my room when Sergei rushes to us, gasping for breath.

"I bring dire news," he says, nearly doubled over with exertion. "The empress just received word. Prussia has attacked Austria. They've taken Saxony. And as expected, England has abandoned them, siding with Prussia."

Peter smiles, clapping. "Brilliant!"

I shake my head. "What is the empress' response?"

He stands tall, leveling a gaze at me. "She has sent a letter of support to Austria. And she plans to dispatch twenty thousand troops to their aid."

"We must stop her," Peter says. "We must intervene before the message can be sent."

Sergei frowns. "It's too late. She sent riders only now with her official offer of support, one to France and one to Austria. King Fredrick has declared war, and we find ourselves on the wrong side."

"I will go and speak to her," Peter says boldly, releasing me. "This matter will be rectified, by any means necessary."

With that, he takes his leave, his men following at his heels. Mikhail spares me a defeated glance before joining Peter. He knows as well as I that once the decision has been made in her mind, there can be no changing it. The deed is done, and we have failed. All that can be done now is to manage the consequences.

"Is Edward still in the palace?" I ask quickly. Though I don't recall seeing him at the theater, I doubt him to be the sort of man to slink away in the night.

"Yes," Sergei says. "He's been taken to the cells. The first prisoner of war. Though, because he is so close to the throne, I suspect he will be released fairly quickly and sent back to England."

"They why imprison him at all?" I ask.

Sergei's mouth twitches. "I suspect the empress is feeling a bit... betrayed. It's something she does not take lightly to."

I nod. Of course. Vanity to the last.

"I would see him," I say, motioning for Grigori to join me.

"Are you sure that's wise?" Sergei asks. "What have you to gain from this? It's too late to prevent the treaty with Austria."

That makes me pause. "That reminds me; send a letter to my mother. Tell her of this unfortunate news, and tell her that, while I love her dearly, I am of Russia, and must act in the best interest of my nation. Tell her that any payments she received from the empress or myself must come to an end, for now, lest they be seen as an attempt to abed the enemy. And tell her that if the situation becomes dire, that my brother and sister may join me here in Russia, for their safety."

Sergei smirks. "You would leave your mother without income?"

I wave my hand. "She is not without resources. If she hadn't been plotting with Fredrick in the first place, this never would have happened. She may fall on the mercy of her co-conspirator if she must, for I find myself completely without sympathy for her. If my brother is willing, I would see him safely out of the grasp of my enemies—including my mother."

I lower my voice. "For all I know, Fredrick had my father killed out of malice. If he wanted my brother dead as well, he would have done it then. No, something tells me Fredrick has plans for my family yet, and to maintain any hope of friendship from me, it is in his best interest to keep my brother safe."

With that, I head for the side staircase and the narrow red carpet that leads down to the small cells that few even know exist beneath the grand palace.

The cells are little more than a row of dull, damp stone tunnels carved into the bowels of the palace. Heavy, iron gates close off some, a few are even beyond that, with thick, wooden doors and only a small,

SHERRY FICKLIN

square slide in the center where one might look upon
the incarcerated. There is a narrow hallway, patrolled
by two guards at all times, even when there are no
prisoners inside. But I don't see any guards now. The
place is eerily still, the only sound a trickle of water
as it seeps from the walls and rolls to the ground. As
I pass one of the heavy, wooden doors, my curiosity
piques. If I opened the small view port, would I see
young Ivan, a boy of only ten years old, deformed and
crippled by growing up in this dark abyss? Would he
be mad, or worse, would there only be a tiny corpse
where he once laid?

I try to swallow, but it sticks in my throat. No,
even in her rage, I could not imagine Empress
Elizabeth being so cruel, not to a child. Perhaps it is
as the rumors suggest, that she spirited the child into
hiding, giving him over to a peasant family who knew
nothing of his birth, or lineage.

At the end of the tunnel, in the very last cell, I see
a flicker of candlelight, and as I approach, low voices
murmur.

I pause, grabbing the lantern from the hook on
the wall and slowly creeping around the corner. Part
of me is bracing for the image of Peter, slicing bits off
The Duke of York, as he'd once done to Bestuzhev. And
as horrible as that might be, what I see is somehow
even worse. Once my mind makes full sense of it, the
lantern falls from my fingers and shatters to the floor
at my feet.

Chapter

TWELVE

I ndignation fills me.

"What is this?" I demand, and the three men jump to their feet. The guards bow deeply, but Edward simply holds up his shackled hands, still grasping the playing cards, and smiles impishly.

"Your Grace," he says formally, inclining his head.

Between them, a small table is covered in fine food, wine, and coins. Playing cards are spread about haphazardly.

"Are you *gambling* with him?" I ask, and the guards mutter yes in shame. "You realize this man is a prisoner of war?" They stand, blinking and gaping at me.

"Your Grace, he is a royal prisoner and—"

I cut them off. "A royal prisoner? No, he is merely the cousin of the king, not nearly enough title to be considered a royal prisoner, to be sure. If he were the heir, perhaps, but he is not. He also stands guilty of attempted regicide."

Now Edward's grin falters.

"We know you were conspiring to assassinate the Queen of Austria during her visit to court. There is a witness."

He lifts his chin, shaking his head. "What witness do you have against me? Some poor servant girl? No word will be as respected as mine."

Now it's my turn to offer him a haughty smile. "I am the witness, Duke. And I assure you, everyone will believe *my* honest word."

He frowns, and I know I have him, so I press on. "The only decision now is whether to send you to Queen Maria's court to stand trial, or to simply hold you here, until we have time to investigate the other charges."

"What other charges?" he demands.

I take a deep breath, hoping he can't read my deceit. "Letters have recently been uncovered that suggest King Fredrick planned to release Ivan and use the boy to take the empress's throne. In the letters, they mention a spy in Russian court, someone who planned to steal the boy and rush him back to Prussia. You wouldn't know who that spy is, *would you?*"

He pales, his eyes widening. "No. I swear I had no knowledge of such a plot. On my honor," he says honestly.

I just stare at him blankly. I know well that the spy was my own mother, but that he doesn't share that knowledge is exactly the leverage I need. "I believe you, on that count at least. But it will be another thing to convince the empress. She is enraged by your betrayal," I lie smoothly. "She wants to see you hanged."

I motion to the guards. "Best not let her find him like this. Remove all this and put him in a cell like a proper prisoner. He will eat the cracked wheat and cream like all the others. No special treatment is to be shown. Is that clear?"

The guards bow again, scurrying off to remove the platters of food and clean up the money. Once they are gone, I step closer to Edward.

"I would ask a question of you. Take care how you respond. If I believe you, I will intervene on your behalf. Perhaps I can convince the empress to send you back to England, rather than watch you swing."

He lowers his head, looking at me as if seeing me clearly for the first time. "Ask anything," he says slowly.

"Are you a man of your word? A man of honor? Bound to the service of your king?"

He licks his lips. "I am, in every way. My loyalty is to my king and my country."

"Good. Disloyal men are of no use to me."

He blinks, looking as if my words surprised him.

"Loyalty is a rare creature in court, as is honesty. You have given me honesty, and so I give it to you in return. I disagree with my empress on this matter. I would see Russia aligned with Prussia and England on this. But it is not my right, nor my place, to make those decisions. Not yet. But someday, God willing,

Peter will be emperor, and he will have the power to choose Russia's alliances. He has great love for Prussia, that much is no secret. But should Frederic ever turn against England, and you'd be a fool to imagine that he wouldn't, you will want someone to advocate on your king's behalf—someone with the ear, if not the heart, of Russia. I could be that advocate."

Edward takes a long, deep breath, as if considering my words. "And what would this friendship cost me?"

"Nothing. Not now. I would only ask, that should the need ever arise, you would do the same, act as advocate on Russia's behalf. I do not ask you to spy for me, or to betray your king, or anything so vulgar. I ask for friendship. That is all."

"And in exchange for my word of friendship, you will be sure the empress sends me back to England?"

I nod.

"Then you have my word. I will be a good and loyal friend to Russia, when the time arrives. And I shall be in your personal debt as well, Your Grace."

"I take you at your word, Edward, and I give mine in return. I will go now and speak to the empress. Hopefully, we can settle the matter and see you safely home very soon."

I turn to leave, my skirts brushing the stone floor with a swish. Behind me, one of the guards pulls the wooden door closed, and I hear the metallic click as the lock falls into place.

I'm nearly up the stairs before I run into a frantic

Peter. His hand is white on the hilt of the small sword at his hip, his green velvet jacket buttoned haphazardly over a rumpled shirt.

"She won't see me! Can you believe that? She refuses an audience." He points over my shoulder. "I'm going to go find that English bastard and rend the flesh from his bones for this."

Gently, I take his free hand and bring it to my lips as I curtsy. The gesture unnerves him so thoroughly that he doesn't challenge me as I turn him around and lead him back up the stairs.

"The guards are preparing him for the rack as we speak, on the empress's orders. He will suffer dearly for his crimes, of that I'm sure. But for now, I think we should discuss our next move. I need your strategic mind, Peter. I cannot figure this out alone," I say, trying to let my voice quiver just a bit.

"Of course," he says, patting my hand and letting me guide him up stairs and to the library. When we arrive, I motion for Grigori to leave us and close the door.

Once we are alone, Peter turns to me, his expression placid. "The solution is quite clear, my Catherine. We must kill the empress."

Chapter
THIRTEEN

I 'm honestly not sure which shocks me more, his declaration to murder the empress or his referring to me as *his Catherine*. Both are so foreign in my mind that a short laugh escapes my mouth before I can stop it.

"No, Peter. You can't be serious."

He pulls out a chair and motions for me to sit, so I obey. "I am very serious. She has obviously lost her senses. Surely, you must see that. She has become a puppet, at the mercy and control of whatever man happens to be sharing her bed."

I shake my head. "If that were true, she would have signed the treaty with England." I regret the words as soon as I speak them because he glares coldly at me. I lower my chin, but continue. "No, Empress Elizabeth is many things, but easily swayed is not one of them."

He flops into a chair across from me, looking more like a petulant child throwing a tantrum than a future king. "Then what do you suggest?"

"Your time on the throne is coming," I assure

him. "What you need to be doing now is making alliances of your own. We will return to Oranienbaum, set up our own court. We will invite heads of state, representatives from all the major courts of Europe. Build friendships, assemble a network of informants in each court. We should begin laying the groundwork that will cement your ascension to the throne, when the time comes."

He puts his head in his hand, pouting. "Pointless. A king doesn't need friends. He needs an army."

"The army is in the empress's control, Peter. We only have our own guard and the three regiments stationed at Oranienbaum at our disposal."

"All the more reason to kill her," he says flippantly.

I stand. "You must stop saying that. She is your aunt and your regent. I will not allow you to speak in such a way."

He seems amused by this. "Oh, you won't allow me, will you? And what will you do, Little Mother? Send me to bed without my supper? Have me spanked?" He narrows his eyes. "Or will you run off to my aunt and tell her on me? Is that your plan?"

I draw myself up as much as I can. "A reign that begins in murder is destined to end the same way, you know that. Elizabeth was appointed by God, anointed with holy oil, and she is protected by his grace. To harm a regent is to be marred forever in the sight of God and man. I would not see you cursed so, husband." I pause. "Please, Peter. I know you are a man of passion, a man of action, but in this matter, please exercise caution and restraint."

"That faithless Duke of York wasn't afraid of God's wrath when he plotted against the Queen of Austria," he says.

"And I believe that even the plot, the intent of his heart, is enough to curse him and his posterity. But that will only be proven with time." I lean forward, pressing a quick kiss against Peter's forehead. "Besides, I care nothing for him. My worry, my concern, is only for you and your well-being."

He brushes me off. "I won't come to you tonight," he grumbles.

I can only nod and slip from the room, trying not to let him hear the sigh of relief as I leave.

That night, my dreams are filled with darkness. In the first, Peter takes my hand, leading me to the ballroom, which is piled high with dead bodies. He laughs and forces me to dance around the rancid corpses. When I can finally escape, I run through the empty, echoing palace halls and find myself outside a familiar door. I'm not sure why I reach out and push it open, but even as I do, a sense of dread ripples through me.

Alexander turns to face me, as handsome as always, with a tiny bundle cradled in his arms. At first,

I'm relieved to see him, but then I notice something is terribly wrong. His dark eyes are ringed in red and his face is puffy. He holds the tiny bundle out to me and I take it, pulling the soft blanket away with one finger. There's nothing inside the swaddle but a pile of white bones, so small...

I drop the bundle, and it falls to the floor in a heap of dust, filling the room and choking me.

I wake with a start, clutching my hands to my chest. My bedclothes are wet, drenched in sweat, and cling to me uncomfortably. Maria rushes in, still in her nightclothes, with Grigori at her side, his sword drawn. I'm shaking all over, part in chill, part haunted by the terrible images still playing in my mind.

"Your Grace, are you all right?" she asks, rushing to my bedside.

"You were screaming," Grigori says, sweeping through the room, looking under tables and behind my changing screen.

When he finds nothing, he sheaths his sword.

"Night terrors," I say flatly, rubbing my head.

He bows quickly and hurries from the room, back to his post outside my door.

Maria wipes the damp hair back off my forehead. "What do you need?" she asks.

I curl into her arms, nestling my face into the long, black braid draped over her shoulder. She holds me like a child, and I let her, saying nothing as she rocks gently from side to side. I don't cry, though a chasm of pain has opened up inside me. It's so fierce I wonder how I will possibly survive it.

My mind drifts, and suddenly, I'm a little girl again. I've been racing the other children down the road and I've fallen, the stones cutting into my knees and the palms of my hands. I've gone to Father, of course. Limping and holding myself as best as I can so as not to bleed on Mother's good carpet. Seeing me, he kneels, holding his arms out.

I rush to him, burying myself in his rabbit-fur robes as I sob. He lifts my chin up, so that I am looking into his bright green eyes. They are so startling against his dark hair and long, black-and-grey beard that for a moment, I'm lost in them. I wrap my arms around his neck and he carries me to the kitchen, setting me on the table. Beatrice, our cook, steps back, wiping her hands on her stained, white apron.

"What have you gone and done now, Princess?" she scolds.

Father fills a bowl with water from the barrel and brings it over to me, carefully cleaning my wounds with a wet rag while I recount the tale.

"Did you win?" he asks after I finish my story.

I can't help but grin. "I did, Papa. All three races."

"Was it worth it?" he asks next.

I frown. Was it worth it? Was winning worth the pain I was in now? Did all victories come at such an expense?

I nod. "Yes, Papa."

He kisses my forehead. "Good. All better now."

I look down at my legs, still oozing blood, and fresh tears come.

"Why the tears, little one?" he asks.

I sniffle. "It still hurts."

He looks down at me, his expression serious. "Yes, it will hurt for some time. Things have to hurt before they can heal. That is the way of life."

Thinking about him now only intensifies the pain, the ache deep in my heart. My mind reels as I grasp for something—anything—to fill the terrible void. I know what I need, the only thing that can bring me back to myself. Sitting up, I struggle to calm myself, if only outwardly, and dismiss Maria. Once she's gone, I make my way to my window and throw it open, letting the cool night air stir through my room as I don my white cloak and make my way to the secret door.

I tap gently on Sergei's door, and when he answers it, he's in nothing but his breeches, his dark hair rumpled from slumber and his chest bare except for the patch of black curls below his neck. Reaching out, I slide my hand up his chest and push him back so I can enter, drawing the door closed behind me quickly. His room is dark, only the pale moonlight streaming through his window illuminates us as I swiftly untie my robe, letting it pool at my feet, my nightdress quickly following. He doesn't speak as he pulls me to him, pressing our bodies together, and kisses me deeply. I run my hands up the exposed skin of his back, and he moans.

"I was afraid I was dreaming," he whispers into my hair as he lifts me gently, carrying me to his bed.

I rub myself against him, using the steel of his arms and the tenderness of his caress to heal the broken pieces inside myself. "Then let us dream together," I answer, and he lowers himself onto me.

When I wake, I'm back in my room, warm, hazy memories of the night flushing my skin. He'd waited until I fell asleep, and then carried me back to my own bed. I remember him kissing me goodnight. Releasing him had taken all my strength. I desperately wanted to keep him with me, if only a little longer, but I didn't dare. Going to him at all was a risk, but well worth it.

I sit up, feeling better than I have in some time, despite the situation. It's almost a relief, I realize. The war has begun, and there is nothing to do about it now. I feel as if a great weight has been lifted from me. Absently, my hand rubs my flat stomach. I can't help but wonder, if in all the reckless abandon of the night...

I let the thought fade as the cold realization dawns. I will have to take Peter to my bed, and soon. Though the thought makes me ill, I know I must endure. I will close my eyes and pretend its Sergei's hands on my body, his kisses on my lips.

And how it will kill me, how it will kill us both. A ripple of panic slices through me. Not only do I need Sergei, I love him. He is my whole heart now. It's funny how I didn't think it would happen, and yet, there it is. It's fierce and selfish and absolutely true. Bringing my sheet to my mouth, I bite down on it, my silly grin straining the sides of my face.

I love Sergei. And I must tell him. The words are practically bursting from my body right now. I bite down harder, fighting to keep them from exploding out of my mouth.

Maria knocks once before entering with a tray of food. Throwing the covers back, I motion to her.

"Help me dress, quickly. And then tell the stewards to begin packing. We will be leaving for Oranienbaum as soon as possible."

As soon as we have managed to make me presentable, I grab a few bites of food and add to my attire my ruby necklace and the sparkling diamond tiara Peter gave me.

I burst through the doors with more enthusiasm than I've had in a very long time, drawing a sidelong glance from Grigori as he falls in step beside me.

"You look well today, Your Grace."

"Thank you."

"What are your plans for the day?" he asks as I lead him down the hall toward Peter's chamber.

"The day is full of possibilities. Perhaps I shall go for a ride," I decide. "But first, I would speak to my husband."

As soon as I turn the corner, I know something is terribly wrong. Servants stand outside his door, muttering softly. When they see me, they all look away, their expressions turning to stone. The door creaks open and Mikhail steps out, dabbing at the sweat of his brow with a dainty, lace handkerchief. Seeing me, he turns my way, holding out his hands to me.

Closing the distance between us, I rest my palms in his, nervous energy cascading over me. "What is it? What's happened?" I demand before he can even open his mouth.

"Peter is ill. When the servants went to wake him this morning..." He trails off, his creamy, white face turning a sickly shade of green.

A sharp wail comes from the room behind me and I turn, just in time to see Elizavetta, her red hair hanging in wet ropes, her white shift clinging to her voluptuous body. Her face is pale, her eyes set in dark circles. Seeing me, she screams harder, a wordless, guttural sound. Two stewards grab her, one at the shoulders, and another around the waist.

"We must wash you, milady," one of them orders, but she ignores them, fighting to free herself from their grasp.

Her dark, puffy face locks onto mine. "He's dead!" she screams before her eyes roll up into her lids, and she swoons.

I snap back to Mikhail, who is shaking his head.

"No, he's not dead," he says in a rush, his voice quivering. "The empress and the physician are with him now. The empress has ordered the girl be washed down thoroughly, lest the illness spread."

I try to swallow, but my throat has gone dry. Of course, because she was with him last night, sharing his bed. Turning back to the limp girl, I watch as the stewards gather her up and return her to the bath.

"Wash her twice," I say loudly. They pause to look at me. "Scrub her until her skin is pink. Then take her to a cell and watch her closely for a few days to be sure she isn't ill as well. We can take no chances."

Nodding, they close the door and I turn back to Mikhail. "What does the physician say?"

He takes a great, weighted breath. "It looks to be the pox."

I take an involuntary step back, right into Grigori's arms, as I struggle to steady myself. Peter might not be dead yet, but the pox would be as good as a death sentence. It had killed Peter the Second, the last direct male Romanov heir, at the age of fifteen. Claiming royals and common born alike, the disease was completely unstoppable. Overcome with grief and fear, I feel my knees buckle, only Grigori's strong hands keep me from falling to the floor.

Another set of hands takes me, and I look up to see Sergei at my side. His uniform is tight and freshly laundered. His many medals and ribbons are clinging to his chest as he looks down at me, his ocean-green eyes deep and fathomless. For a minute, I'm unable to draw breath. I want to cry or rage, but I'm too numb. The feeling has gone from my arms and legs, and all I feel is a terrible weight on my chest. If Peter should die, my time here would be over. I'd be sent home to my mother, a childless widow, or at best, I'd be sent to a monastery to live out my days in seclusion. Either way, my life at court would be over.

As I hold onto Sergei, I wonder if he would go with me, if we could run away together, if he would have me as his wife, or if he would choose his duty to Russia over me and remain here with the empress. His expression offers me no answer.

The door to Peter's chamber flies open and the empress glides out, a white handkerchief held tightly over her mouth. She narrows her eyes at me and with a silent jerk of her head, demands I follow. Helping me regain my footing, my men, each taking one arm, lead me to her private office. Sitting behind her massive, oak desk, the empress waves the maid over to pour us both a drink. The young girl lifts the teapot to pour, but the empress quickly caps the cup with her hand.

"I think we are going to require something a bit more than tea," she says, and the maid scurries away, the teapot clanking on its silver tray as she moves past me and out the door. Grigori releases me at the door and takes up his post outside. Sergei, however, walks me inside and helps me into a seat across from the empress. She's traded her usual outlandish gown for a simple, silver brocade gown with small panniers and her royal-blue sash. Her dark hair is twisted into a small bun at the back of her head, as if she'd been about to put on a wig, but never got to it. Long, diamond raindrops dangle from her ears as she takes a moment to put her jeweled crown atop her head before speaking to me.

Her cold, blue eyes dart from Sergei to me, and then back to me again. Her lips press down into a thin, disapproving line.

"I need to speak to Catherine alone," she demands, not looking to the handsome man beside me, but keeping fixed in my direction.

He gently drops my hand, stands, and bows deeply from the waist. "Your Majesty, with all due respect, the grand duchess has had quite a shock today and—"

She cuts him off harshly. "The grand duchess doesn't need *you* here to hold her hand. Now do as you are told or I will have you removed."

He hesitates only a heartbeat, as if trying to find words that might soothe her foul temper, but finds nothing. He bows stiffly, and then strides out the door.

She takes a deep breath and makes a sour face. "Notoriously unfaithful creatures, men." She smirks at me. "But I suspect you will find that out soon enough."

I say nothing. My mind churns, trying to come up with reasons she might want me to stay, something— anything—to keep her from sending me back to Prussia today. Without meaning to, I feel my hands glide over my belly, where the dim prospect of being with Sergei's child floats to my mind. If Peter dies, and if I am pregnant again, that would be enough to keep from being dismissed to a convent or sent back to Prussia, at least for a while. But those are both uncertain things, and the uncertainty does not sit well with me.

"What are you thinking?" she asks as the maid returns with a tray of wine and two glasses. The empress dismisses her with a flick of her hand and pours the drinks herself, handing me a glass.

"I was thinking, praying, that Peter might get well," I say, the dishonesty like bitter candy in my mouth.

She leans back, taking a drink. "No, I think you are wondering what to do next to save yourself. You are a great deal like me, you know. Pragmatic." She pauses, setting her glass on the desk. "That's why he likes you. You remind him of me, only younger and more pliable."

I blink.

"Sergei, of course." She folds her hands, fiddling with the rings on her fingers. "He was a young buck when I brought him here, only sixteen and fresh off the battlefield. Still, he was clever and brave and, well, he has other fine assets as well."

I lower my eyes, feeling the blush creep up my neck and into my face.

She continues. "He's quite fond of you. I noticed it right off, though I doubted you returned those feelings, seeing you look at young Alexander the way you did. So perhaps, it was my own doing. Perhaps my sending your boy away is what finally sent you into Sergei's arms. But then, I wondered, could Peter not fulfill his conjugal duties? That would not be terribly surprising, as he has proved to be useless in every other way as well. "

I swallow a long drink of wine but say nothing, letting the sharp warmth roll down my throat, steeling my nerves as it calms my churning belly.

"Either way, Sergei is and will always be mine. You will have to choose another." Her face has gone soft, serene, her voice almost gloating.

I shake my head. "I'm sorry, Your Majesty. I don't understand."

She leans forward, her breasts pressed against the desk so the fabric of her bodice is strained against them, as she slowly explains. "Peter is dying. The pox will take him soon enough, and I will have to go in search of a new heir—a tiring and difficult process at best, I assure you. Or, you will give me my heir."

I frown. She must suspect that I might be with child again. But who would have told her? Grigori? No, surely he would not betray me so. Elizavetta? I would not put it past her, but I can't imagine how she would gain such knowledge.

I set my glass down, mustering up all the courage I have. "And if I am not pregnant?" I ask softly.

She tilts her head to the side. "Then you must

get pregnant. And quickly too. Before Peter dies, you must be with child."

I balk. "I can't be with Peter now, or I will likely take ill as well."

"Stupid girl, must I explain everything?" she says, sitting back and refilling her glass. "Go back to Oranienbaum. I will let it be known that I sent you away because you were once more in a delicate way, and then you must find some way to get the job done. Perhaps you could enlist the help of your new guard. He seems dependable enough, and he's quite nice to look at as well."

I feel my mouth hanging open in complete disbelief at her words. I'm sure I must have misheard or misunderstood. She must read my confusion because she presses on.

"Take Mikhail, if you'd like. He resembles Peter at least, though I'm not sure if he is overly fond of ladies in that respect. Or I could always call your dear Alexander back to court, if you prefer."

The bland audacity of her words finally shakes me from my stupor. I leap to my feet, my gown swishing around my ankles as I take one step forward, pounding my fists on her desk, making her jump in surprise.

"Don't you dare," I shout. "How dare you speak to me like this! I'm not some common whore you can throw into any bed you please in hopes of propagating a child. I'm the future Empress Consort of Russia!"

She stands and slaps me sharply across the face. If she means to bring me to my senses, she's terribly mistaken. Anger froths through me and I open my hand, returning her slap and knocking the crown from her head. It skitters across the floor with a clang.

Righting herself fully, she clutches the side of her face. "How *dare* you raise your hand to me? I am the empress, and you are *nothing*. Any power or title you possess, or may someday possess, are given to you by my hand, and I can have them stripped just as quickly. You stupid, spoiled, selfish girl. I'm talking about the good of the nation here, not your vanity or wounded pride. You will do as you are told. If I want to send you to bed my entire army, you will do it, and without question. Do you understand me?"

I feel the furious pounding of my heart, so loud and strong it reverberates through me like cannon fire. My chest heaves as I struggle to calm myself. "And if Peter lives? If he recovers only to find I am heavy with another man's child? He will kill me with his bare hands," I say honestly. I might have tricked him once, but this could not be hidden or explained. He would know the awful truth, and it would kill him. It would kill us both.

"Peter will do as he is told, just as you will."

It seems her mind is made up on the matter. "And if I refuse?" I ask, my head still high.

"You may be thinking that being sent back to Prussia or off to a nunnery would be preferable to sullying your angelic reputation, but I assure you, what I will do to you if you disappoint me will be nothing so kind. Your mother, after all, came here as a spy and a traitor. Being that she is not here to pay for those crimes, it would fall to you. And, of course, the sentence for treason is death." She taps her fingers on her chin, looking away absently. "I could just lock you up and let you slowly starve to death. I've heard it is a most terrible way to die."

She swings her gaze back to me. "And make no mistake, if you ever lay a hand on me again, that is exactly what will happen, child or no child." Her face is round, puffy, and flushed, the mark of my hand still burning on the side of her face quite visibly.

"I will leave for Oranienbaum tomorrow," I say sternly. She breaks into a pleased grin before I add, "But I'm taking Sergei with me. He may have been yours once, but he is mine now, and believe me when I tell you that I will not leave him to your tender mercies. I think we have both had quite enough of those."

Her face puckers as she mutters, "Take him then."

I curtsy and turn to leave, looking back over my shoulder to add, "And I will see Peter before I leave."

She nods and waves me out. As soon as the door closes behind me, I press my back against it, trembling as I take in a long, deep breath. My face stings from her assault, and my eyes are filled with tears that I fight to hold back. Sergei tips my chin upward, examining my face.

"Are you all right?" he asks, his voice tinged with worry and barely concealed rage.

I push off from the door and start walking. "I should have let Peter kill her when I had the chance," I mutter.

Chapter
FOURTEEN

The kitchens are abnormally quiet. Sergei has gone off to speak with the physician, leaving me in the ever-watchful company of my guard. Not wanting word of Peter's condition to get out, the empress has cancelled the evening's events and sent many of the palace staff home for the day. Besides Grigori and me, only the head cook, Beatrice, remains in the always hot bake room. Over the fire, a venison roast rotates on the spit as she slowly cranks the handle. Her long, sky-blue gown is dirty, stained with soot, flour, and blood. Her apron has caught the brunt of it, but there are two telltale stains where she has wiped her hands on the skirts themselves. Her hair is dull yellow with streaks of silver poking out from her covered bun. Her thin face is flushed, her lips cracked and dry. She eyes me warily as I putter around the kitchen, grabbing bits of dried spices to add to my boiling pot.

When I'd come down to make Peter some soup, she had tried to do it for me, despite being shorthanded, but I waved her off, wanting to do at least one kind, wifely thing for Peter before he met his end.

The bits of rabbit are heavily salted, making the soup too bitter. I gently crush a handful of herbs and release them into the boiling juices, stirring it slowly. Behind me, Beatrice moves swiftly, retrieving a glass bottle from the back of the cupboard and handing it to me.

"Best add a bit of this, Your Grace."

I hold up the jar, trying to determine its contents. Peppercorns, perhaps?

"It's crab eyes. Said to be the best thing for the pox," she adds quietly.

I nod gratefully, not wanting to ask how she knew about Peter's ailment. More likely than not, the servants are already buzzing with news. Heaven knows they can't keep anything a secret for long. I pull the cork and the smell, while not overpowering, is a bit rancid. I shake about half the bottle into the soup, then add some more spices, carrots, and potato chunks for good measure. Replacing the cork, I hand it back to her.

"Best keep some aside, in case anyone else falls ill," I offer.

She nods and returns to her spit. Once the potatoes are tender enough to be crushed with the back of the spoon, I ladle some into a bowl and put it on a tray. Turning to take it up the stairs, I'm intercepted by Grigori, spotless as always in his dark green uniform that matches almost perfectly the shade of his eyes, his dark, wavy hair restrained with a ribbon at the back of his neck. He takes the tray briskly.

"Allow me to carry that, Your Grace."

I nod and lead him toward Peter's room. Along the way, I am stared at by everyone from servants to grooms to visiting nobles. I feel their eyes on me as if I were naked, heavy with pity and shock. I nod cordially as I pass, both to servant and noble alike, my back straight, chin high, a soft smile that is kind yet meek plastered to my face. I will show no fear, no weakness, as I can afford neither, despite my internal struggle.

The empress has given me her blessing to be with Sergei, at least privately. Far from the prying eyes of Winter Palace court, I can continue my affair, discreetly, of course, as I choose. Provided it produces an heir. If it does not, she will call me unfaithful, treacherous, and whatever else she can think of to punish me. If I succeed, she will likely allow me to remain in residence at Oranienbaum until the child comes, and possibly after as well. There will be no returning to Prussia, no convent. I will live comfortably as mother to the heir, and perhaps even have leave to remarry, eventually.

I'm standing outside Peter's door when I shake myself from my thoughts. Guilt rushes in, hard and cold. What sort of wife am I? Half planning for, but also half wishing for, my husband's death? I take a breath, murmuring a quick prayer for forgiveness for my errant thoughts, and then another for Peter's speedy recovery. I nod to his valet, who opens the door for me, handing me a scrap of white, cotton fabric to tie around my nose and mouth before I enter. I do it quickly, and then take the tray from Grigori.

"Wait here," I order. He nods, but looks warily at me. I'm sure he would rather I flee at once than risk myself, but I owe Peter this much, this little bit of comfort I can offer. He had, after all, been at my side after I was poisoned, and again after my fall. He had nursed me and worried over me more than once.

I step inside and there is a nurse with a similar cloth covering her mouth, gently changing the damp cloth laid across his forehead. His eyes are closed, thank heavens. I don't think I could have hidden my expression of horror without a moment to adjust to the sight of him. His hands lay at his sides, so swollen and blistered that they don't even look human. A blotchy rash crawls up the collar of his shirt and spills across his chin and jaw, up his cheeks to just below his eyes. His lips are swollen and bright red as if he has painted them with strawberry juice. When the nurse places the rag on his skin, he hisses, as if it burns. When he opens his eyes, I'm standing there, barely having regained my composure.

"You should go," he says hoarsely, licking his lips.

I lower my chin and force a reassuring smile. "Nonsense. I've made you some soup. It should ease your discomfort." I pause. "A bit, at least."

His head rolls from side to side. "Go. Unless you've come to kill me, then go now."

"Of course I haven't come to kill you. That's the fever talking. Here," I sit in the empty chair at his bedside, fill a spoon with broth, and hold it over his mouth. "Try this. I have it on good authority that this soup could very well cure you of this illness."

He gives a laughing cough but opens his mouth enough for me to dribble the liquid down his throat. I fill another spoonful and repeat the process over and over until all the broth is gone, leaving the vegetables in the bottom of the bowl. I've even managed to get him to swallow a few crab eyes. When I set the bowl down, he looks at me sternly.

"Why have you come?" he asks, his voice soft but a bit stronger.

I look away, not wanting to meet his gaze as I impart my news. "The empress is sending me away, back to Oranienbaum. She wants me away until you are well again."

"Until I die you mean." He coughs again, and the pain of it makes his hands spasm.

"I will defy her, if you wish. I will stay here, by your side, if you want me to." The moment the words escape my mouth, I taste the truth of them. I would stay, if he asked me to. Out of duty and obligation, and perhaps, something more. "She would never force me to leave if you demanded I stay. She's never been particularly good at refusing you, for any reason," I add with a sly smile.

Of course, staying, should he perish, would mean signing my own death warrant. Somehow, looking at my once-handsome prince, it feels like a perfectly reasonable risk to take.

"Go," he mutters. "Go and do your best. Prepare our court as you said. Invite nobles, entertain diplomats, and make Oranienbaum our seat of power. Because if I survive this, we will need allies. Make sure the soldiers are training daily. Work them hard. But," he pauses, taking a rattling breath, "take Elizavetta with you. I know how you hate her, but she is dear to me."

It feels as if he's slapped me, and it hurts much more than when the empress did it in reality. I frown. "If she's not ill, I will take her back to Oranienbaum," I promise. I don't add that she will be mucking out horse stalls and washing floors for the rest of her days.

He nods and slips into a deep, hopefully painless, sleep.

Gathering myself, I leave the room, yanking off my makeshift mask as soon as the door is closed, and then crossing the hall to the bath were a basin of hot water waits. I wash myself well, scrubbing my skin until I'm red and raw. The nerve of him, asking me to care for his mistress. In a fit of anger, I lash out, toppling the brass basin and its soapy contents to the floor. Grigori appears at the door and holds out a towel, which I take and dry myself with quickly.

"Is everything all right?" he asks.

I turn to him, my tone accusing. "Did you hear? He wants me to look after his mistress. The woman who—" I catch myself just in time, before I can explode with rage and let the accusations boil from my mouth. "When the empress and I were shouting earlier. Did you hear what she said to me?"

He blushes, but holds my eyes, nodding slowly.

"Did you hear what she said about you? About how I should take you to my bed?" My voice is high and frantic, my emotions raw and painful. In that moment, I'm not sure if he deserves my rage or not, but he's there and that alone makes him a target.

"I did," he says softly.

"It's not enough that my husband is a faithless bastard, that I've had to sell my soul to survive between them, but now I'm to be her whore in the quest for an heir." I step close to him, so close I can feel the heat of his breath against my face. He's a hair taller than I am, but I draw myself up as fully as I can, challenge in my voice. "Will I never be free of this sin, this shame?"

His eyes widen in shock, but I'm unable to bring myself to reason. "What can I do? What would you do, if such a demand were made upon you?"

He looks at me for a moment, his expression wavering, and then steps back. "Your Grace, I would do anything you ordered of me, anything I could to ease your suffering, but..."

I'm not sure which makes me angrier, his easy

agreement or his hesitation. "But what?"

"But I would not wish to be with a woman who did not care for me, who did not, in some way at least, love me, and who I did not love in return. You, at least, care for... him."

Though he doesn't say Sergei's name, his message is clear. I do care for Sergei, but in being ordered to his bed, she had made our connection less somehow. Something tawdry. I have to turn away to hide the hurt I'm feeling. It's enough to double me over, an ache in my stomach so deep and so raw it drives the air from my lungs. He reaches out, but I wave him off.

"I need a moment to compose myself," I say shakily. I can almost hear Sergei's voice in my head.

What do you want? it demands.

I don't know.

That's not good enough. Decide what you want.

What do I want? I want to stay in Russia, preferably as Empress Consort, but I would settle for being the mother of the future king. They are the only safe choices.

What do you need to do to get what you want?

I chew at my lower lip. I need to do as Peter says, go and solidify our court at Oranienbaum. And I also need to produce an heir, if possible.

I turn, straightening myself as best I can. "I apologize for my outburst. It was uncalled for. I would never ask such things of you, nor should I be discussing these matters with you now." I pause. He nods, so I continue. "It has been a very stressful day. Perhaps I will go for that ride after all. Please go to the groom and have him prepare our horses. And while you are down there, please have one of the stewards fetch Elizavetta from the cells. See that she is packed and ready to travel by morning. She can walk behind the carriage," I add with a bitter smirk.

The ride is long and hard and by the time we reach the river, my hands ache from holding the reins so tightly. I slip from my horse and take off my gloves, walking to the beach. I hear Grigori dismount behind me, his steps never far behind mine.

The air is chilly as the sun begins to set on the horizon, lighting the sky with violent shades of red and orange as if it's been lit on fire. Kneeling, I dip my fingers in the cool water and rub them together.

"Do you think the grand duke will die?" he asks. It's extremely inappropriate, a very personal conversation to be having. But I suppose after my own inappropriate conversation, the wall of propriety between us is slowly being dismantled.

"I don't know. I hope not, but then, so many do. Peter was never vigorous as it was. Even as a boy, his health was often poor. I can't imagine how he would have the strength to survive," I answer honestly.

Grigori slips off his sword and sits down, balancing

the blade in his lap. "What will you do?" he asks, further testing his boundaries.

I know I should reproach him, but it feels so good to have a confidante again, it's hard to bring myself to the task. Once it had been Sergei I talked with, but now that option seems very far away. Curse Elizabeth for souring him for me.

"I will do what I always do, my very best." He reaches out to grasp a stone to skip across the water, and his uniform lets out a loud rip as the shoulder tears free. A nearly frantic chuckle escapes my lips. "I suppose my first order of business will be to redesign your uniforms."

He laughs too, and it's a warm, friendly sound. "I might be able to offer some suggestions on that front, though I am no tailor."

"I would hope so," I say, sitting not far from him. "We will begin hosting visitors immediately. We'll have to have an occasion of some kind."

"The white nights are coming," he offers.

The white nights are those rare days when the sun never fully sets, plunging the countryside into a state of perpetual twilight.

"That might do nicely. Three days' worth of events. We will send invitations to every noble, every tradesman, and every envoy in Europe. It will be expensive." I tap my fingers on the ground as ideas roll through my mind like the waves along the shore. "But we will have a few months to plan, to send invitations.

Yes, that will do nicely. And in the meantime, I will take a lesson from the empress' example. The nights at Oranienbaum will be filled with frivolity and amusement."

"And the days?" he asks, dusting off his breeches as he stands, offering me a hand.

I take it and let him help me to my feet. "Strategy, politics, and, if we are very lucky, security."

By the time we reach the palace stables, night has fallen in earnest and the lamps are being lit around the great hall. Maria greets me at the entrance, taking my gloves and hat.

"We are packed and prepared to leave, Your Grace. The carriage will be here by midday," she says, her tone excited.

"Happy to be leaving, are you dear?" I ask pleasantly, taking her arm.

She nods. "Happy to be going home, Your Grace."

"Good. There are some matters we must discuss, delicate matters that must be kept in strict confidence. Can I trust that to you?"

She turns and curtsies. "Of course, Your Grace."

Her voice is sincere. I know that unlike the other ladies in my entourage, she isn't a gossip, and she's not prone to flights of fancy or romantic notions. She's rock solid, a Scottish lady who was sent to Paris, and then here to me after some unwanted attentions from a very married duke. Some might think her gruff for a young woman, but I see it for what it is—a quiet dignity.

I don't tell her the worst of it, of my forced infidelity and the empress' plan to secure an heir, but I tell her that we must leave due to the possibility that I may be with child. I tell her about my hope for Peter's recovery and my plans to elevate Oranienbaum from a simple country palace to an Imperial Court to rival even Empress Elizabeth's.

"We must be cunning," I say quietly as we lean over my ivory and ebony chessboard. "We will need to secure alliances of our own, and find those in rival courts who might act in our interests. Beginning here. When Peter recovers, I will see him one of the most powerful, respected men in all of Europe."

She nods, moving her queen to take my rook. "There is a maid, she isn't one of the empress' ladies, but she tends to them. She overhears a good deal of their talk, and I happen to know her husband has a taste for expensive spirits."

I grin, looking at my dark-haired companion. She's plain, not unsightly, but not a stunning beauty either. Yet there is wisdom behind her eyes, dark like those of a young doe, which makes me see why the French duke was so taken with her.

"Then, before we go, you shall speak with her, offer her a few coins and a few choice bottles from Peter's private stock. I would like her to keep her ears open for anything to do directly with Peter and myself, General Salkov, or our Prussian neighbors. Make sure she knows there will be more available with any worthy news I receive from her." I take her queen with my bishop. "And check."

"Will you see the grand duke again before we leave?" she asks, conceding the game gracefully.

I hadn't planned on it, truthfully, but thinking of it now, I think I will. I would like to say goodbye, and perhaps, to offer forgiveness while I still have the opportunity, lest the worst should happen. If there is one thing I have learned, it is that forgiving others is worth more to the weight of one's heart than being forgiven oneself.

"I believe I shall. In the morning. Will you help me prepare for bed?"

She nods and follows me to my private chamber. Freed from the riding habit I'd still been wearing, I change into a fresh shift and crawl into my bed.

Hours later, when the lamps have died and the palace is plunged into darkness, I sit upright. My mind is brimming with plans, things I must do, people I must see, far too busy to allow me the respite of sleep. Putting on my cloak, I step carefully into the outer chamber and light the single candle on my writing desk, settling myself in to begin what I know will be a tedious task of making a list of people to call to court. My eyes squint in the dim, flickering glow, but my hand flies across the parchment as if possessed. I never hear Sergei enter the room through my secret passage. I don't feel him standing behind me as I usually might; I'm far too distracted for that.

It isn't until I feel his lips on my neck, the gentle prickle of his chin stubble across my tender skin, that my fingers release the quill and I turn to him. "Any news from the physician?" I ask, my voice colder than I expect.

"Nothing new. Peter's symptoms are worsening, though that is to be expected now. It will be a miracle if he survives."

I jerk away from his touch. The last thing I need is yet another reminder of what I have lost, and what I must do now. It's not that I dislike the idea of being with Sergei, quite the opposite, it's only that I don't like being ordered to do it. Perhaps it's silly to quibble about it, but there it is all the same.

"Are you angry? Have I done something?" he asks, taking a cautious step back.

Turning in the chair, I look him over. He's as handsome as ever, his broad chest pressing against his shirt, stretching his royal-blue vest taut. He's changed since I saw him earlier. His hair is combed back harshly against his scalp, his medals replaced by a simple red sash.

I frown, my mind instantly suspicious. "Why have you changed?"

He looks down at himself. "There was a bit of an accident. The empress spilled a glass of wine on me earlier."

My mouth goes dry. Of course she did. "And I'm

sure she was all too happy to help you out of your soiled clothes as well."

He opens his mouth to speak, but I wave him off. "No, don't say anything. I'm sorry. I have no right to lay claim to you. You aren't my husband or my property." I'm unable to keep the misery of the truth from my voice. "I'm only glad to know that you cared to be in my bed *before* you were forced to be there by Her Majesty."

Stepping forward once more, he lifts my chin. "I'm neither of those things, but I am yours, nonetheless. And not by force, but by choice."

Unable to stop myself, I stand and press against him, grateful for the darkness and our brief seclusion. I stretch up on my toes and kiss him, drawing him down to me with my hands locked behind his neck. He responds, but hesitantly.

"I love you," I whisper against his lips. I feel the restraint seep from his muscles as he snakes his arms around me and clutches me to him, kissing me deeply, thoroughly, and in ways that make my skin burn.

He pulls back, a devilish grin on his face. "Is that jealousy I taste on your lips, princess?"

I look down, straightening his jacket. "Yes, it is. I just don't understand."

With one finger, he tips my chin up again, forcing me to meet his eyes. "What don't you understand?"

I shake my head. "You loved her once. Maybe you still do. I don't understand how you could have. She can be so cruel."

His smile falters. "I don't think it was love. Infatuation, perhaps, that grew into admiration, respect. But never love."

"How do you know the difference?" I ask earnestly.

He takes my hands, pressing them to his chest. "To love someone is to put them first, above everything else. Above duty, honor, and responsibility. That was never the case with us. We were a convenience to each other, nothing more. She wanted a child, and I wanted to be a general. Sad, but true."

I frown. "And yet, she remained childless."

He nods. "She did. And as we have recently discovered, the issue was not on my part."

In a flash, my nightmare returns and I have to push the images away. "She's jealous. She doesn't want to let you go. She is sly and cunning and she will take you from me if she can." I wrest free of his arms. "Only today, she demanded I take another to my bed, an army of men if so needed, anything to produce an heir. She would have offered me to anyone, save you."

Now he shakes his head, pulling me back into his arms. "Is that what troubles you so?"

"And why wouldn't it? She has demanded I whore myself for her cause. It was only after I struck her that she agreed to let me take you back to Oranienbaum."

His mouth turns up in a smile. "You struck her? For me?"

I nod, folding my arms over my chest.

He licks his lips, choosing his next words very carefully, "Is that not why you came to me, that first time on your wedding night? In order to produce an heir?"

I think about that for a moment, trying to decide what to say. "No. If you had sent me away, refused me, then I would have gone back and met my fate with the empress. I would not have sought out anyone else. I didn't come to you because I needed someone in my bed. I came to you for comfort, kindness, and hope. You gave me all of those things." I take a breath, not wanting to hear the answer to my next question, but knowing I must ask it anyway. "If you thought so little of me, thought I was the sort of woman who would use you so terribly, why did you allow it? Why did you not just send me away? Was it pity? Duty?"

Anger flashes across his face as he grabs me. He kisses me again. This time, it's hard and fierce, his lips crushing themselves against mine ferociously before pulling back just enough to keep our foreheads pressed together.

"I was intrigued by you at the first, that day in the snow, your knife in hand to defend yourself and your mother. But then, I watched you. You met every challenge; you succeeded when so many others would have cried for mercy or faltered under the strain. It was your courage that caught me, and it was your honesty and grace that kept me. When you came to me, it was a gift, a miracle. I would have taken you in any way you could have given yourself to me. I still would. Never assume that I consider you a harlot for the choices you've made, because that is far from the case. You are my angel. I only meant that this decree changes nothing between us."

Guilt weighs on me like stones in my heart. Here I am, fretting that by giving her consent, nay, her order that I be with Sergei, we are somehow lessened. But in truth, it is a gift. I can give myself to him without fear of her reprisal, as long as it gives her what she wants. Does that absolve me of my greater sin, the sin of loving and giving myself to someone other than my husband? I do not know. Looking into his eyes now, I don't know if I care.

"If she orders you to stay, will you?" I ask, trying to hide the desperation in my voice.

"No," he says flatly. "She may try to seduce me, she may even threaten me, but I will not stay with her. I will not abandon you, not now, not ever. Because I put you first, always. He touches my stomach reverently. "But what if I fail you?" he asks quietly. "What if I cannot give you another child?"

I frown. Having conceived with him before, the possibility had scarcely crossed my mind. He must sense my confusion because he continues.

"Today, when I refused her advances, she said..." He takes a deep breath as if the words were bitter in his mouth. "She said that if I cannot give you a child, and quickly, she will send another man to your bed."

I cannot hide the shock and outrage from my face. "I would not allow it," I say sternly.

He lowers his face and for the first time ever, I see him waver, his expression filling with something so like fear that it chills me. "I would understand if you did. If you had to. I think I might die from the pain, but I would understand."

Taking his hands in mine, I walk backward, leading us slowly to my private chamber. "We may not be wed in the eyes of God, but in my heart, I am your wife and so long as you live, I will never give myself willingly to another. Not to save the empress, the dynasty, or even my own life. Do you believe me?"

He nods solemnly.

I tug on him gently. "Good, then come be with me now. Not for the sake of a child, but so that I might enjoy you for myself alone."

Dawn breaks far too soon, and I wake to an empty bed. With the help of Maria and the maids, I wash and dress quickly. I eat only a meager breakfast as the last of my belongings are put in trunks for my journey.

I make my way to Peter's room only to be refused at the door.

"The fever has worsened," the valet says nervously. "I can hear him screaming and raging through the door. The physician says no one must be allowed in."

"But I am his wife," I demand.

As if to prove a point, Peter screams, a string of obscenities echoing down the hall. The young valet blushes but I push past him, cracking the door.

"Peter, it's Catherine. I'm preparing to leave and I wondered if I might come say goodbye?"

The room stills, and finally, he says in a calm voice. "Come in, but keep behind the screen."

I slip inside and a tall, wide screen painted with a dense jungle scene divides the room. I cannot see his bed, but behind the screen, there is a chair, and the empress sits in it, her wide, golden gown sticking out on either side. In her hand is a small, lace fan, her hair covered by a tall, white, curled wig, and her face is powdered snow white.

I hadn't planned to see the empress before I took my leave, but now I have no choice. I force myself into a deep curtsy. "Your Majesty."

"Good. You're here. I've been explaining to my dear nephew the precarious position his illness has put us in. You especially. Isn't that so, Peter?"

On the other side of the screen, he screams again, this time insulting us both in the most colorful ways.

The empress fans herself, unimpressed by his tantrum.

"Are you mad?" I demand. "He's ill, and you sit there tormenting him. Do you want him to die?"

She glares. That's when I realize she is not alone at all. Sergei steps out from the back of the room and into my sight. He looks pale, uncomfortable, and even a bit angry judging by the clench in his jaw. I look back to the empress, who is smirking.

The revulsion begins in my stomach and flows up, into my chest and throat like bile. I manage with great effort to hold my tongue despite the names I would like to call her myself.

Ignoring her, I walk forward, grabbing onto the screen. "Peter, I'm so sorry. I know that isn't enough, but it is true nonetheless. And I hope you get well very soon and come home to Oranienbaum."

I wait for his rage, for the names and the vulgarity, but none come. He says nothing. His silence is perhaps a better judgment than his anger, I realize, stepping back. I will never forgive him his crimes, and he will never forgive me mine. We are damned, the two of us, and it is much too late for redemption.

I turn back to the empress. "We are leaving," I say, motioning to Sergei. My voice drops to a whisper. "You know, my father told me something once when I was just a girl, learning to hunt. He said, *never wound anything you don't intend to kill.* Good advice, that."

She looks at me in surprise, blinking quickly as if trying to determine whether my words are a threat. I smile sweetly and curtsy, taking Sergei's arm as we head for the carriages.

Chapter

FIFTEEN

The ride goes quickly with Maria and my other ladies sharing my carriage. They are excited to be going back, and their giddiness is contagious, despite my precarious situation. Behind us, Grigori and Sergei lead the guards and the rest of our procession. I'd even taken mercy of Elizavetta, who looked battered and half-starved after only a day in the cells, and let her make the journey on horseback.

The carriage rolls to a stop at the front entrance to the tall, golden-yellow palace, between the two massive, gold fountains. It's perhaps half the size of the Winter Palace, but no less grand. The palace staff stands in the courtyard, their clothes flapping in the strong breeze, as my carriage door is opened and I step out into the evening glow. With my ladies behind me, I stride into the palace, inhaling deeply. It smells of lavender thanks to the nearby fields, and it's warmer than Winter Palace, giving it a relaxing feel. I strip off my gloves and hat, setting them on a silver tray near the entrance.

The palace hasn't changed at all in my short absence, but there is something about it that I struggle to put my finger on. I wander aimlessly through the French doors and into the grand parlor. The walls are light sage-green with pink trim, murals of cherubic hosts in each wall panel. Tall ivory and marble statues and busts surround me, the Greek gods and goddesses. The parquet floor makes a hollow sound under my feet and I glide my hands along the wall until I reach the far window, which overlooks the massive gardens. Closing my eyes, I know what has changed.

It's me.

I'm not sure when I came to think of Oranienbaum as my home, certainly not during my miserable nights of being locked in my chamber with Peter, but only more recently. Perhaps it was my distance that made my heart yearn to be back here, far from the ever-watchful eye of the empress and her army of lovers and spies. And now, now with Peter gone and my would-be chaperones called away, it is mine completely. Every bright corridor, every fountain, every finely decorated alcove belongs to me. I turn and make for my room, enjoying the feel of the mahogany banister under my bare hand as I climb the stairs. Every servant I see greets me warmly with a bow or curtsy. There is no judgment in their faces, no hard edge of anxiety in their posture. There is a simplicity, a stillness, which welcomes me into its arms like a loving parent.

For the first time in a very long time, I am home.

The maids unpack my things slowly and carefully as I allow myself a long soak in a hot bath. When I dismiss my servants for the night, I send Grigori off as well. There is no danger for me here, at least none that requires him to stand watch at my door through the night. Maria brings me up a cup of fresh milk and helps me into bed. By the time Sergei finds his way into my room, I'm bone tired. I don't send him away, but rather curl myself up against his warm skin. He's hot as an oven hearth and somehow soft and strong all at the same time. But I haven't the energy to be amorous, so I allow myself to drift to sleep in the warmth of his arms.

I don't wake again until late the next morning, long after he has snuck back to his own room. When Maria enters to help me dress, I know I'm going to have to tell her about Sergei, and the full measure of the empress' demands. Keeping such an affair would be too exhausting, and with Peter gone, the full measure of running our young court falls directly on my shoulders.

If she is shocked by my revelation, she hides it well, her expression remaining passive as I explain.

"You can be assured of my discretion, Your Grace. And you have my sympathies as well. What a terrible position you find yourself in." Her voice is unwavering, strong, and I have no doubt she will do as she says.

I nod, both in acceptance of her sympathy and in acknowledgement of her vow. "It is a dangerous, precarious position, to be sure. But," I pause, thinking of Sergei, "perhaps not so terrible."

While we eat breakfast, Maria helps me make some notes on everything from the need to bring in more cooks into the kitchens to the state of the apple trees in the orchard. As we plan, I feel full of hope and wonder at the prospect of my new undertaking, and also a bit overwhelmed by the sheer enormity of it all. Peter, while often leaving matters of court unattended, employed a bevy of advisors who dealt with most of these things, but I want to be more hands on. I want people to come to know that I am the ruler of this palace, the Grand Duchess of Oranienbaum Court in every way. Of course, I will need some assistance if I'm to truly make Oranienbaum independent from the empress' court. We will need to have our own treasury, our own supplies, and for that, I must convince the Privy Council to support me. I don't want to be reliant on Empress Elizabeth in any way. For her, I want it to seem as if we do not exist, let me and my palace slip from her mind as much as is possible. That is my goal now.

My first order of business to attend is gathering the lords for a Privy Council meeting. Most of them know me well enough, as I've often sat in for Peter when he was too drunk or simply too uninterested to attend. Convincing them to support me fully in Peter's indefinite absence, however, will be a more difficult task.

Sitting behind Peter's desk, I begin making the customary invitations and announcements. I will have to hold an open court in Peter's absence as well, a time for the peasants to be able to come forward and have their grievances settled. There will be taxes to be collected soon, and I'm eager to hear how the people in the village are faring now that the fever has passed through.

I will also need to see to the guards, to inspect the regiments as Peter would demand, and see to the new uniforms. Drawing a folder of notes from Peter's desk, I see stacks of unpaid bills, orders, and a multitude of other issues I will need to deal with as well. I sigh deeply, an ache forming behind my eyes as I start making stacks.

A knock at the door shakes me from my thoughts. "Come in," I call, not looking up from my neat stacks.

"Your Grace." It's Sergei's sweet tenor voice. I'd know it anywhere, and the sides of my mouth twitch up at just the sound of it. "May I be of any assistance?"

I put down what I'm working on, offering him a smile. "That would be lovely," I say. "Could you begin by calling for some wine and asking the court secretary and the financier to join me as well?"

He nods, a wry smile spreading across his face.

"And Sergei, I need the architect as well. I find myself in need of an office of my own." I pause, picking up the thin lead shaft that holds Peter's royal seal. I suspend it in my fingers, rolling it back and forth. "And I will need my own seal."

❧

It takes seven weeks before Oranienbaum Palace falls into a blissful, if busy routine. My days are eaten up with meetings, negotiations, budget discussions, and civil hearings. Serfs who might normally travel to the Winter Palace to seek justice or ask for assistance now come to me in open court. It is a delicate balance, appeasing both the lords and the peasants alike. Whenever a particularly difficult situation arises, I take a recess to convene and seek wisdom from the Privy Council. While I don't always accept their advice, simply asking for it ingratiates them to me.

Sometimes, however, answers are not easily found.

"I am saying that if you open up the royal gardens to every hungry peasant, we will be overrun and we will have no food left for ourselves," Sergei growls, raking his hands through his dark hair.

I shake my head. My crown feels abnormally heavy today, the weight of it making my temples pound like hammers on an anvil. "So you would have me let this man and his family starve? This man who has been a loyal subject, who has plowed our fields since he was a boy, I'm to send him away hungry? No. We have lost too much already. The fever decimated the serfs working the land here; we can't afford to lose any more able bodies."

"So you will feed him today. What about next month, and the month after? What is your solution? To allow him to continue to take more than his share? What will the others serfs say? How long will it be before they come knocking, looking for a handout as well?"

I stand, moving around the desk in a soft swish of skirts. He stiffens when I touch his face. He's cross with me. His cheeks are flaming hot and his face flushed. My hand feels like ice against his skin but I hold it there, as if I can cool his temper just by touching him.

"Sergei, my wise advisor. I understand your concerns. But know this, I will not send this man away hungry. I will not send him to starve. So what is my option? Please, help me find another way." I speak slowly, calmly, and as I do, I can feel the fury fading from him. His tight mouth softens into a hint of a smile, his body relaxes and the tension leaves him in a long exhale. Taking my hand in his, he kisses my palm.

"Yes, I'm sorry. You have a good heart, which is one of the things that draws people to you, your sense of fairness and your love for your people. I know you will not turn your back on anyone in need. It's just, I cannot think of what can be done for this man and his family." His expression is tired. It's been a trying day and we still have to greet a new guest to court, Lord and Lady DuMonlac, a Parisian envoy and his wife.

I step back, walking to the window as I search my mind. Tapping the glass with my fingers, I play various scenarios through my head. Sergei is right about just handing the man a bushel of grain. During the height of the fever, we'd been able to assist by allowing the people to repay debts once they were well again, but now, this man was unable not only to repay what he'd borrowed, but had nothing to feed his wife and young sons either. He says his wheat crop failed from disease while he was too ill to tend it. The lord of the land says the man is lazy and often behind in his rents and wants to see the man jailed for non-payment.

There's a knock on the door, and my steward enters cautiously. "Your Grace, it's time."

I nod and make my way past Sergei.

"What are you going to do?" he asks, catching my arm as I pass.

I tug myself free gently. "What I was born to do, rule."

And with that, I return to the main chamber. Trumpets blare and the steward announces me. Sergei follows me in, taking up a seat in the aisle with the rest of the lords and ladies, and I take my seat in Peter's red-and-gold throne.

The man, Stevn Eildenson, steps forward and drops to one knee in front of me.

"I have taken some time to consider your request. Lord Galtin has requested you be jailed; you have asked to borrow more food. I am denying both requests." A soft murmur ripples through the assembly, which I silence with a sweeping glare. "However, Lord Galtin is within his rights as land owner to remove you from his land, and I am granting him that. It seems to me that you are a poor farmer, either through bad luck or laziness, I do not know, but he is hereby granted leave to seize the lands and place new serfs in your place."

The man doesn't look up, but I see him wobble and falter, falling to the floor on his other knee as well, clutching his worn hat to his chest, which is shaking with silent cries. "But I am not heartless. I know you, and the others serfs, have suffered much this season. As it happens, I have a few openings for kitchen staff. Your wife can cook, I imagine?"

He lifts his head, his dirty face streaked from the tears, but there is a hint of hope in his expression as he answers shakily, "Yes, Your Grace. My Lilia is a wonder in the kitchen."

I nod. "Good. I would have her join my staff here, and your sons might find positions as cupbearers as well. And perhaps, if you are willing to attempt a new vocation, the stable master might be in need of someone to help clean the stalls. You will, of course, find housing in the palace staff apartments."

Now he's nodding furiously, twisting his hat in his cracked hands. "Yes, Your Grace, of course. Thank you, Your Grace."

I hold up a hand. "But I warn you now, you will find that I am a taskmaster to rival any lord, and you will work here, because if you do not, if you waste my mercy, you will regret it. Do you understand?"

He nods again, this time lunging forward. My guards leap to stop him, but I wave them back. Taking the hem of my gown in his hands so carefully you'd think it made of silver rather than sturdy cotton, he lowers his head and kisses the hem before crawling back.

"God bless you, Your Grace."

I glance over to Lord Galtin, who nods approvingly.

"Excellent. Who is next?" I say, taking a long drink of the glass of wine my steward holds out to me.

That night, I spend longer than usual at the chapel. As always, I say a prayer for Peter and his recovery. Though I have been writing to him daily, I'm unsure if he's receiving my messages because he never responds. It's possible that he's too ill, though my spy among the maids tells me his condition is much unchanged. I pray for strength, wisdom, patience, and for the safety of my family far away. The war between Prussia and Austria rages far from my quiet palace, but the news my guests bring to my ears is always the same. Great battles, much bloodshed, and little hope of an end in sight, they say. I mutter a prayer for an end to the conflict, a prayer for peace. I say a prayer for the child that I lost, and a prayer that I might finally be with child again, and then I head to the ball already in progress.

The steward announces me and, as has become our tradition, Sergei escorts me in. Tonight's masquerade is a vision of pure decadence. On an elevated stage in the center of the ballroom, various acts perform. One large man is juggling knives, another is spitting fire into the air, and a third, a woman, is bending herself in all manner of unseemly ways. The performers are a gift from the Lord and Lady DuMonlac. Lady DuMonlac is a cousin of the French king's notorious mistress, and she is watching the show with rapt attention while her husband flirts with some of the other ladies of court. The ball had been Sergei's idea, based on something very popular that Empress Elizabeth did on occasion. Tonight, all the men wore massive gowns, corsets, and tall, powdered wigs while the ladies donned pants and suits. I glance at Sergei, who kisses my hand before releasing me into the crowd. Somehow, even in white powder makeup, his dark eyes ringed with kohl and his lips painted the deepest red, he is still devastatingly handsome. I watch him raise the black lace mask to his eyes and then fade into the crowd.

Before I can collect myself, a figure appears before me, bowing formally.

"Your Grace, may I have this dance?"

I frown, the voice is familiar, to be sure, but between the gown, the makeup, and the mask, I can't place who it belongs to. Without waiting for my answer, he takes my hand and leads me to the dance floor. We dance in silence for some time. All the while, I'm trying desperately to figure out my partner's identity. The song ends and a wave of excited chatter fills the hall. Around us, people begin laughing and pointing up. The performers have taken to the sky on hanging trapeze wires and swing back and forth over our heads. All eyes are on the spectacle so no one sees my dance partner take my arm. He jerks his head, a silent plea to follow him from the room to a nearby balcony.

Licking my lips, I nod. I'm not sure who this familiar man is, but I'm burning with curiosity. As soon as we are out of sight, he turns, stepping close and stealing a kiss.

The moment our lips touch, I jerk back, my hand slicking through the air like a sword and slapping him in the face hard enough to knock off his black, satin mask.

"How dare you?" I demand.

He rights himself, holding the side of his face as it reddens. "Not the welcome I was hoping for," Alexander says with a grin, even as his green eyes glisten with tears of pain.

I can feel the anger rolling off me in waves. "What are you doing here?" I demand loudly, smoothing my hands down my bodice.

His smile falters immediately, and he holds a

scrap of paper out to me. I snatch it from his hands and turn my back as I read it.

"She summoned you," I say, balling the paper in my hands angrily. Turning back to him, I throw the letter over the balcony. "The empress sent for you. Did she tell you why? Or were you so eager to return that you didn't even ask?"

He takes a step back and bows deeply. "I'm sorry for startling you. Truly. But we traveled a long way to come to your side and—"

I cut him off. "We? We who?"

For the first time, he looks truly uncomfortable as he rakes a hand through his dark hair and down the back of his neck. He hasn't changed at all since the last time I saw him. His face is perfectly preserved in my memory, and other than a dark hint of beard growing across his chin, he is exactly the same. Frozen in time.

"Rina came with me. She is going to have the baby any day and I couldn't bear to leave them, but the empress insisted I come," he admits finally.

I suck in a breath. Rina, my friend. She is here, fat with child, under my roof. How is it possible to love and loathe someone at the same time? That is the ache in my heart when I see her, when I see either of them.

I laugh dryly. "And did the empress tell you why she wanted you here so desperately? Did she inform you of the task she expects you to provide?"

He frowns, and I know she has. He knows why

he's here—it's why he came. The empress expects me to bed Alexander while his pregnant wife sleeps down the hall. The depravity of it makes my skin crawl. He must see the indignation building inside me because he steps forward, reaching out to me.

I step back, out of his grasp.

"Don't touch me," I order. "Whatever you think is going to happen here, whatever task the empress assigned you, will not come to fruition. Do you hear me? I'm not a whore!"

My words are too loud and carry too much weight. I can feel partygoers begin to look my direction, wondering what is happening. Looking over my shoulder, I see my guard takes his place behind me, mostly blocking me from view. I take a deep breath and lower my voice.

"Go home, Alexander. I don't need you here, I don't want you here, and I refuse to use you as breeding stock for the empress." My heart is heavy as I speak the words. Even though they are true, sending him away—again—is surprisingly difficult.

"That's what you have Sergei for, is that right?" he snaps, his tongue sharp and his tone cutting.

I look down, knowing I cannot meet his eyes. "I love him. I've found some small measure of happiness here. But seeing you, it's like a wound being re-opened. I didn't want her to send for you, she did it to spite me, to cause me pain because I've failed to provide her with an heir. If Peter dies and there is no heir, she will kill me. She's told me as much. So I will do what I can, have my joy now, while it lasts."

He reaches for me again and this time, I don't move away. He holds my arms gently.

"I didn't come here to hurt you. I didn't even come here to bed you. Whatever the empress might demand of me, I am not a man who could betray my wife so. I came—we came—because we were afraid for you. You're right, the empress is desperate, and that means you are in danger. I couldn't let you face that alone."

I look up at him, trying not to think about his hands on my skin or the warmth of his breath. I will not think of those things. "I'm not alone. As you said, I have Sergei. How did you know about that, by the way?"

He shrugs. "Rumor and innuendo. It's difficult to keep secrets at court."

I clench my jaw. "That is a lesson I learned all too well, I'm afraid."

He frowns but says nothing.

"Is everything all right?" Sergei asks as he walks up behind me.

Alexander releases me and steps back, nodding to the taller man.

"Fine. The empress has sent Alexander and Rina to join us here at court. He was just making his presence known."

"Is that so?"

The tension between them is thick, stifling. I take

Sergei by the arm. "Come dance with me."

He bows and takes my hand, wrapping it across his arm. I pause, looking back over my shoulder. "And Alexander, if you ever try to kiss me again, I'll have you whipped," I say flatly before gently tugging Sergei forward onto the dance floor.

Chapter SIXTEEN

Later that night, I'm sitting at my vanity brushing my hair when Marie lets Sergei into my chamber before excusing herself for the night. He walks up behind me and runs his fingers through the loose tresses. I let my eyes flutter closed as the sensation relaxes me.

"I wasn't sure I should come," he says in a low whisper, making my eyes fly open.

"Why not?" I ask, catching his hand and kissing it gently.

He turns, pacing over to my bed and taking a seat on the edge. His face is twisted in grief, and it took me a moment to understand the source of his worry since he would not speak the words.

"You were afraid Alexander would be here, weren't you?" It's not an accusation, but he looks away in shame.

I set my heavy brush down and walk over to him. "I told him to leave." Running my fingers through his hair, I gently tug his face upward so he is looking full at me. "He won't, of course—he won't risk angering the empress by disobeying her—but he knows nothing will happen between us. I told him I love you."

I expect joy, or something akin to it, but his expression is sour and he nuzzles his head into my belly.

"Perhaps you shouldn't send him away. Perhaps..."

I push him away. "Perhaps what?"

He holds his hands up as if they will shield him from me. "I'm just saying that, well, you aren't with child."

I feel my mouth perk up. "Not for lack of trying."

He smiles sadly before continuing. "Yes. But the fact remains that as long as you remain childless, you are vulnerable. Goodness knows it looks as if the boy has no issues in that department. His young bride was with child fast enough."

His words hit me like a blow to the stomach. Not untrue, but painful all the same. I recoil and he shakes his head, taking my hands and drawing me back to him.

"I'm sorry. That was tactless. But I'm worried for you. And if seeing you secure means..." He doesn't finish the thought, but he doesn't have to.

"And you would happily see me in another man's bed to make that happen?" I say, unable to believe what he's suggesting. "Why not? Let's call him in. Shall we call in the guards and the stable boys as well? They can take turns with me until I'm good and fat with child. Is that what you want?"

I can't keep the anger and disgust from my voice, even as it trembles. I feel the tears behind my eyes, fighting for release, but I hold them at bay.

He stands, clutching my face in his hands. "How could you say that to me? The idea of anyone else touching you, it makes me ill. I want to murder someone. But I don't want to lose you just because I'm too weak to share you."

Lowering his head, he kisses me and it's brutal, full of pain and rage as his teeth and tongue tear at my mouth. When I finally pull away, my lips throb from the abuse. I grab the front of his shirt, balling it into my fist, pulling him to me until we are nose to nose.

"Listen to me, Lord Salkov. I am the ruler here and you are *mine*. There will be no other man in my bed or in my heart so long as you are in this world, so do not even think of asking me to be with someone else ever again. My decisions are my own to make, and you will not pass me off just to absolve your own misplaced guilt. And if I'm never blessed to carry your child again, then I will go to my fate knowing that I had this time, however brief it may be, with the man I love. And if you ever speak to me like this again, I will have you shackled to my bed, is that clear?"

He nods wordlessly.

"Good. Then do as your princess commands, and kiss me."

He obeys.

Later, as we lie in bed, he kisses my forehead.

"I'm sorry," he whispers.

I nuzzle against him, playing with the small patch of dark curls in the center of his chest. "No. There's nothing to be sorry about," I say, not wanting to spoil the moment.

But he's not to be stopped. "When I saw him on the balcony, with his hands on you, I thought my heart had stopped beating."

Propping myself up on one elbow, I run my fingers up and down his bare chest. "How many times must I say I love you before you will believe me?" I ask.

He catches my hand. "I know you love me. But he was your first love, and that's something not to be underestimated. First love is the most dangerous."

I tilt my head to the side. "What do you mean by dangerous?"

He licks his lips. "I mean that first love never really goes away. Even when you move on, there is this connection, this bond. It's unbreakable. That's what makes it so dangerous, because you will always feel it, even when you don't want to."

"You sound like you're speaking from experience," I say. When he doesn't answer, I ask, "Elizabeth was your first love, wasn't she? That's why you stayed even after."

He nods, entwining his fingers and mine. "I thought it was love, at the time." Suddenly, I know his feelings all too well. The hatred and jealousy I felt seeing him in the empress' chambers as she tried to seduce him, how desperately I wanted to kill her in that moment. That's how he feels now. And I am helpless to make it better.

Maria bursts into the room, and I lurch upright in bed.

She curtsies. "I'm so sorry, Your Grace, but you are requested urgently. There is a message from the empress. And also, Lady Mananov has gone into labor."

Dressing as quickly as possible, I go to Rina first. The empress' letter will no doubt confirm that Peter has died and will either be calling me back to court or will have instructions for my exile. Either way, they could wait.

With Sergei and Grigori at my side, I approach her chambers. Alexander is leaning against the wall, gnawing on the nail of his thumb while her screams echo down the hall. Seeing me, he stands, bowing deeply.

"What does the midwife say?" I ask, slipping off my long, satin gloves and donning the white apron the nurse has provided.

"Nothing. We had only woken when the bleeding started. By the time the midwife arrived, Rina could no longer stand. She's so pale..." His voice trails off, his eyes distant.

Back home in Prussia, I'd attended only two births, one of a new colt and the other, the daughter of a maid. Both were bloody, exhausting, and stressful. More than enough to terrify any sane person. But both were successful nonetheless. And this would be as well.

Leaving the men at the door, I enter the room. The midwife looks up.

"Pardon me for not dipping, Your Grace, but the babe is struggling something awful. You probably shouldn't be here for this."

I move to Rina's side and take her clammy hand. Her long, blonde hair hangs in damp strings, and sweat covers every inch of her. Her face is pallid and hollow and her breathing labored as she tosses and turns against the pale white sheets. Around us, the maids scurry about in silence, taking away blood-soaked towels and bringing clean ones. Finally, after what feels like hours, the midwife leans forward across Rina's limp body and speaks to me in hushed tones.

"The babe needs to be turned, Your Grace. It's dangerous for the babe and the mum, but I might lose them both if I don't try." Her voice is heavy and her tone clipped.

The words surprise me. Surely, she can't be leaving the decision to me? I look down at Rina. Even in this moment of terror, she looks fiercely determined. She whispers just loud enough for me to hear, her voice dry with exertion. "Save the baby."

I wipe her forehead. "We will save you both," I

promise and nod to the midwife, who goes about her task with startling brutality.

Rina screams again and several things happen at once. The midwife steps back, her arm bloody to the elbow, and orders the maids and me to lift Rina to her feet. We heft her, and I rub her lower back. The midwife sits on a stool in front of Rina, tearing away the front of her bedclothes. In the next moment, the babe slides free and Rina slumps against us. The air thickens around me as we lay her back carefully and the room grows eerily still. For a moment, it's as if time has slowed to a near stop. On the mantle, the gold and tortoiseshell bracket clock ticks like the beat of a dying heart. Each breath I draw is labored and achingly shallow. Glancing over, I see the midwife holding the child, rubbing it this way and that, tugging gently on its small arms and legs. Finally, it lets out a wail, loud and strong, and it's as if the entire room takes a collective breath of relief. Turning back to Rina, I watch her eyes flutter closed.

"Rina?" I shake her gently.

"She's all right," the maid assures me, waving me aside and covering her in clean blankets. "Just exhausted."

The midwife stands, bringing the baby over. It's not crying anymore, just making soft cooing noises. She looks down and sees Rina sleeping.

"Would you like to present the babe to his father?" she asks, holding the tiny bundle out to me. My throat is too dry to respond. Part of me wants to never look at the creature, but there is a deeper part, a maternal instinct perhaps, that demands I take the child. She lays the infant in my arm and something falters inside me, a resentment I didn't realize I'd been clinging to falls away like a veil, and it's as if a ray of sunshine is beaming directly into me. The child blinks up at me with clear, dark blue eyes, and yawns, its tiny, perfect mouth forming a little O before drifting off to sleep. There is a hint of fuzz-like black hair crowning its head and as I hold him, something else becomes very clear.

"Is everything all right Your Grace?" The midwife asks, puzzled by my expression. I smile, stroking the tiny hand with one finger.

"I was just thinking that everything is as it should be," I answer more to the child than her.

When I step through the door, Alexander rushes forward and I smile, both to reassure him and because I simply cannot contain the joy of it all.

"Congratulations, Lord Mananov, you have a son." I hold the bundle out to him, and he accepts it awkwardly.

"A son," he murmurs, transfixed by the tiny face.

"And Rina is well also. She is just resting now. You can see her if you'd like," I say, moving to Sergei and winding my fingers through his.

Alexander looks up at me, his expression unreadable, but a smile on his lips. "Thank you."

I nod and slip out of my apron, tossing it in a ball beside the door as he slinks inside. As soon as the corridor is empty, Sergei leans down and kisses my forehead.

"What are you thinking about?" he asks.

I turn to him, frowning. "I'm thinking how lovely it must be to have a simple, uncomplicated life. I'm thinking that they will raise that beautiful child together. They get to be a family."

I can't keep the sadness from my voice. "It's a bittersweet thing, to have been unsuccessful in our attempts to conceive again. I want nothing more than to carry your son, to bring him into the world and hold him in my arms. But to have him raised here, a pawn of the empress, for you to never be able to hold him like a proud father and claim him as your own, I think that would have been misery for both of us."

He kisses me again, this time on the lips. I sigh against his mouth and he pulls away.

"Well, are you going to open it?" Sergei asks impatiently.

My eyes slide over to the letter, still sealed with red wax and Empress Elizabeth's unmistakable emblem. I stuff my quill into the inkwell and sit back. "Yes. Eventually. I want to make sure a few more items are tended to before I lose the authority to do anything at all." My chest is heavy as the realization of my situation comes full fold. I glance up and his eyes are on mine, his thoughts unreadable as always. I wonder if he will come with me, if I'm sent away as a penniless widow. Perhaps he would leave Russia and come to Prussia with me, and we could marry there. Or perhaps he will want to return to Winter Palace and the empress' side. If I'm to be sent to a convent, I wonder if he would help me steal away. We could flee to the mountains, disappear...

I shake the thoughts away.

"What is so important?" he asks.

I lift a handful of papers recently delivered to me by my privy council. "There's a chapel two towns over that needs to be rebuilt after a fire last month. Also, the lower town needs more grains and the well in the east village has dried up. A new well must be dug to supply the town with water. And then there's the matter of the mill—"

He sits back, effectively silencing me with a sharp glare.

I sigh, resigned. "Fine."

Picking up the letter, I round the desk and lean against the front of it, snapping the seal with my thumbs and carefully unfolding the paper. As soon as the words are read, the air rushes from my lungs and the parchment slips from my fingers, fluttering to the floor.

"What is it?" Sergei demands.

I can't speak, the shock is nearly paralyzing. Swallowing, I shake my head.

Snatching the paper from the floor, he skims it quickly, reading aloud as he does so. "...pleased to inform you that the grand duke is expected to make a full recovery."

His head snaps up. "This is what you hoped for, isn't it?"

I can't think clearly. Hadn't I wanted Peter to live? Yes and no. I'd rather grown accustomed to the idea of leaving court, or perhaps even remarrying. I'd been carefully planning and plotting, trying to prepare myself for every eventuality. But now, all that was dashed to hell. I hadn't even imagined a miraculous recovery was possible, hadn't dared let myself hope for it. Now I can feel myself flushing and my mind reels, grasping for a plan, a next step that will put the ground under my feet once again.

"Yes, of course. He will come back here." I feel the words slip out, but I can't remember deciding to speak them.

"The empress says he should be well enough to travel next week. We should make arrangements."

I nod slowly, rounding the desk and returning to my seat. "I must make arrangements." I lick my lips, hesitant to speak my next words but finally gathering my wits. "You realize there can be no more we, not like there has been recently. Peter will move back into our apartments and..."

I trail off. What more is there to say? My husband is returning.

"You will still need an heir," Sergei says pointedly.

I look up and realize I've hurt him. "I don't mean to give you up, my love. Never that. I only meant that we must go back to being extremely discreet. No more staying all night, no more affection in public. The servants will be gossiping and while I didn't mind so much before when I thought," I pause, drawing a breath. "I would not have Peter find out. For both our sakes."

He nods, and it takes all I have not to go to him, to find comfort in his arms. But Peter is returning, and I know I will have to learn to find my solace elsewhere.

Chapter
SEVENTEEN

T he days fly past as we prepare for Peter's return. The entire palace is on alert as every detail is tended to with absolute precision. We send for the finest wines and entertainers. I prepare a small tournament in his honor filled with the sport of old days, swordplay, jousting, and archery. When he arrives, the garrison will perform a formal drill and then stand inspection for him. He will be told the new uniforms were made as a special honor to him, and I pray he will believe that small lie.

Even as everything comes together, I feel myself weakening. The exertion and pressure is nearly debilitating and on the day of his arrival, I have a fit of dizziness that nearly takes me to my knees. The silver, diamond tiara is heavy on my head, and it's only with Maria's support that I make it to the welcoming procession at all. The breeze feels good against my skin, crisp and cool, a sure sign that summer is coming to an end.

From my left, Elizavetta approaches, her hands

folded demurely in front of her. As she approaches me, her head down, her petal pink gown flapping in the breeze, I realize I haven't seen her for weeks, during which she's been relegated to serving as a maid for my most pious of visiting noblewomen, Lady Jane Faust. They've spent countless hours in attendance at the chapel, reciting biblical verse, or in silent prayer. I smirk at the thought. Perhaps a little piety is exactly what she needed because as she approaches me now, her expression is meek, shamed even.

"Your Grace," she says with a deep curtsy.

I nod to her, and she rises. I want to release my grudge against her, but I find myself unable. Though I cannot be sure of it, I still suspect she pushed me down the stairs and killed my unborn child, and that suspicion grows like a noxious weed in my heart. Walking slowly, she takes her place in the rear of the procession and Maria squeezes my arm, pointing to the gates in the distance.

"He's here," she says jubilantly.

I wave my hand and the trumpets sound, drums beat, flags bearing the Romanov crest flap gently, and the thunder of hooves grow louder as the carriages and horsemen approach. The gold gilt carriage rolls to a stop, and the footman rushes to open the door. When Peter steps out, all the anxiety, all the weariness, rushes inward, stealing the air from my lungs.

His cane hits the ground with a hollow sound as he slowly marches forward. His face is pallid and scarred terribly, welts left behind from the pox. His head is covered with a powdered wig with long, white rings up the sides. Though his caftan is light blue like the sky and covered in silver lace and diamonds, it looks too large for his frail body. It's as if he's aged twenty years in only a few months. I step forward, dipping in to a curtsy to greet him. Behind me, the rest of the court follows suit.

"Peter, welcome home," I say warmly.

He rushes past me, nearly knocking me aside. I expect him to run into Elizavetta's waiting arms, but he shuns her as well, hobbling as fast as his still-weak legs will carry him into the palace. He doesn't pause to greet his lords or to wave to the assembly, but rather he climbs the stairs like a man possessed. I quickly thank the nobles for attending before following him to his office.

"Peter, is everything all right?" I ask, closing the door behind me.

"Get out," he says calmly before sorting through the stacks of books on his shelf.

"What are you looking for?" I ask. "Is there something I can—"

He cuts me off. "No. Just leave."

I nod and turn to go. He isn't upset it seems, only eagerly distracted. Pausing, I look back over my shoulder. "There is to be a feast tonight to celebrate your return. Will you attend?"

He throws the book he's holding onto the floor.

"Why wouldn't I? You think I'm too ashamed for people to see me like this?"

Realizing too late that I've upset him, I scramble to ease his temper. "Of course not. I'm so relieved you are well and returned to us." I take a breath. "It's only that I can imagine how lonely you've been, and I wondered if you planned to spend the evening with Elizavetta."

When he glances up at me, his eyes are earnest. "Who?"

My mouth falls open, and I stammer. "Your mistress."

He chuckles and waves me off. "Of course not. I see that Alexander is back in residence. Your idea, I suppose?"

It feels as if I'm standing on a great precipice, my footing unsure. "He is returned, at the empress' request, not mine, I swear."

He shrugs. "Good. It will be nice to have my friends at my side once more." Apparently finding what he was looking for, he holds up a thick volume and makes a victorious grunt. As he slips past me, he gives me a quick peck on the cheek, which I am far too stunned to return. "Go see to the feast preparations then, wife. There's work to be done. I'll see you tonight."

He could not have shocked me more if he'd pulled a pheasant from his pants. I stumble into the hallway and watch as he walks away, his gait encumbered but swift as his cane slicks against the parquet floor. A familiar face appears at my side. Mikhail, ever Peter's doppelganger, is taking in the scene. I turn to him.

"What's going on?" I demand.

He frowns, not looking at me as he whispers, "I have grave news. I think Peter means to kill the empress."

I'm pacing in my office, only Grigori and Mikhail watching me with wary eyes as I chew the nail of my thumb. "I don't understand. She was supposed to be caring for him," I mutter.

"Oh, she did," Mikhail assures me, rubbing his bloodshot eyes with the mounds of his palms. "She never left his side, even in the worst of it. She ate, slept, and even insisted she hold all her council meetings in the adjoining chamber."

I take a deep breath, closing my eyes.

"He got your letters; she read them to him every day," he adds.

I shake my head. "Then what's going on? I can't possibly believe he's had a change of character. Is such a thing even possible?" Could I dare let myself hope that at some point, in the height of his illness, he found peace and forgiveness in his heart? Or had the fever addled his mind so badly that his memories had been washed away?

"I don't think that at all, Your Grace. From what I

observed, he was constantly muttering, writing notes in the air as if to remind himself of things. He seemed to grow stronger in his resentment each day."

I frown, pausing near my window where the rising moon shone low and large in the dim twilight sky, its pearl glow reflecting in the calm water of the river.

"I suspect that he was plotting, growing resolved in his anger. One day I was sitting with him when the empress was holding council. It was impossible not to overhear."

"What did you hear?" I ask, not bothering to tear my gaze from the distant water.

"The empress said that it might be better if he died, then she could name your unborn child as her successor. She said that even if he survived, she planned to pass him over and make your child emperor. She said he was too twisted and grotesque to ever rule a nation."

I let my eyes flutter closed. The empress, with one careless conversation, pushed Peter into a state of mind I'd never thought him capable. Violent, yes, he could always be that, but never calculated, never methodical. I'd honestly wondered if he had the intellect to be devious. Well, now I had my answer.

"She's created her own destruction," I say, turning to Mikhail, who nods in agreement.

"Surely you can say something, advocate reason?"

I laugh, and it's a dull, rueful sound. "When has Peter ever been open to reason? No, there is nothing I can say to change his mind on this."

"It's treason, Catherine. If he's discovered to be plotting some madness, she will have to kill him. She may well decide to kill you both," he pleads.

I don't think he's ever called me by name before, I'm not sure I condone the informality of it, but we are discussing my husband's potential treason as if it's afternoon tea, so I suppose it's acceptable.

I lick my lips. "I will try. I can promise no more. But if I discover evidence of a plot, you must know my duty is to report it to the empress."

He frowns. "You would sacrifice your husband so boldly?"

Looking him directly in the eye, I nod. "I would. Because if Peter is so far gone that he cannot see reason, I would not risk seeing a crown on his head either."

With a curt bow, Mikhail turns to leave. With his hand on the door, he pauses, turning back to me. "What I don't understand is, with Peter ill, how could the empress possibly hope that you might be with child? Are you?"

My back goes rigid under the scrutiny of his words. "No, though I'm sure she had a plan for that as well."

He glances at me, his expression one of pity and understanding. There are few people on this earth who know the depravity that those in power are capable of, and he is among them. Perhaps, in some small way, that makes us allies.

When he leaves my office, I return to my window,

twisting my wedding ring around my finger. As it moves across my skin, I swear it tightens like a noose around my neck.

Chapter
EIGHTEEN

The feast that night is flawless, and I can't seem to relax enough to enjoy it. I try making introductions to Peter of the visiting nobles, but he is uninterested. While people dance, he sits on his throne beside me and scribbles notes on parchment. I try to glance over and get a peek, but it looks like gibberish. When I spot Elizavetta in the crowd, I gesture for her to come over and greet him, but he will have none of it, waving her off without once even looking up. His shaggy, blond hair is longer now, unruly and falling into his eyes so that he has to continually wipe it away.

"Would you care to dance, husband?" I ask, trying to catch his attention. He looks up at me and, for the briefest of moments, I see something flicker in his expression, something dangerous.

"Not tonight." Setting the parchment and quill aside, he stands. The music fades to a close and trumpets sound. "People of Oranienbaum, what a feast we've had. I have been gone far too long from my palace. I know many of you thought I would never return, but God has spared my life so that I may take my place as Emperor of Russia. So be thankful, praise His will, and marvel at the miracle of my survival. The days of feasting are only beginning," he says, lifting his goblet of wine high into the air.

The assembly cheers and the music resumes.

"I'm glad to see you in such good spirits," I say, taking a drink.

He frowns. "There is much to do and little time to accomplish things. You have done an adequate job of managing the palace affairs in my absence, but I am returned now. I have a great deal of work to attend, but first, I think I must speak to you privately."

In the crowd, I spot Sergei chatting with one of the nobles and I nod, taking another drink of wine before accepting Peter's arm and allowing him to lead me from the room. There is a calmness to him that unnerves me. He's like the river, still on the surface but churning beneath the tranquil façade.

Without a word, he leads me to our chambers. He stops Grigori at the door. "You, guard. We have no need of you this evening." Peter dismisses him. His eyes flicker to me, and I nod as imperceptibly as I can. Though the last thing I want is to be completely alone with my husband, I know well that he can much more easily take out his aggression on my guard—possibly even kill him—for disobedience.

Once inside, I pour a glass of brandy and hand it to him. I had prepared as best I could for this possibility once I knew he was returning, but even now, my nerves beat at my stomach like butterfly wings. He accepts the glass but doesn't drink, setting it on the table beside him instead. Moving in close, he makes a *turn around* gesture with his finger. I turn my back to him and he reaches up, tugging my perfectly tied hair free. It cascades down my back in dark waves as he rakes his fingers through it. My entire body is shaking, not with desire but with a deep, instinctual fear. It's as if I'm a cornered animal, and he is a predator coming for me.

"I did as you asked, while you were ill." I'm stammering, but the tension is so thick and consuming I'll try just about anything to distract him. "I looked after the palace, put emissaries and spies in place, invited lords and ladies to curry favor. Many of the nobles have been coming to us rather than the empress."

I feel his hands slide down my back and begin fumbling with the laces of my gown.

"With you, you mean. The nobles have been coming to you."

I open my mouth to protest, but he grips the shoulders of my gown and rips it from my back, over my shoulders, and then releases the scraps of fabric to the floor.

"I wondered at first how you would get them to trust you." He pauses, one hand running down the side of my corset, the other snaking around my waist and pulling me against him. "How many of them did you have to bed to gain their loyalty? One? One hundred?"

I gasp in a shallow breath. "None, of course none. Why would you think—?"

He cuts me off by drawing a long knife from his belt. I feel it slide past my hip as he brings it up so I can see it, pointing the tip at my face. "She told me why she sent you away. What orders you were under." His voice hisses between his teeth and into my ear.

"Then you know what she demanded of me. I had no choice but to take someone." I falter, realizing I've already said enough to condemn myself. "She even sent Alexander here hoping that I would... but I didn't. I refused."

My heart pounds so hard I think I might faint.

"So you took a lover?" he asks, drawing the blade of his knife up my side.

"I did," I whisper. "Only one."

"Who?" he demands. "Tell me."

I shake my head. "I will not."

I feel the knife slice through the back of my corset in a rush of cold steel. It falls free, and I'm left shaking in only my sheer, pale shift. "You will tell me or I will kill every man, woman, and child in this palace."

"You wouldn't," I say, not entirely sure I can doubt his words.

He sighs. "No, I really wouldn't. But I will kill some, people close to you."

He circles around me, never really releasing me but still keeping me at a distance. I set my jaw defiantly.

He tsks at my refusal to respond. "Fine. Then answer me this, are you pregnant?"

I swallow, and it feels like I've got something stuck in my throat when I speak. "No."

"Good. I would have killed you and the bastard; I want you to know that." He looks at me as if I should be pleased that he's decided to spare my life. "As it is, the empress plots against me. Against us. She may still try to choose a new heir; I know she is searching for options. She doesn't think I'm pretty enough for the appointment anymore," he says, motioning to his scarred face.

"It's not so bad," I whisper and he lashes out, slapping me with such force that I fall back and into the table, barely managing to keep my feet.

"I'm hideous. But I'm also strong. Much stronger than I was before. I see what's happening around me, I see everything. I'm like a *god* now."

I feel my eyes widen at his delusional proclamation.

Reaching down, he takes me by the hair, lifting me upright. "But there's a plan for me. I see it now. So much work to be done. And one thing I still require of you."

"What?" I ask, feeling my strength return. The fear is fading now, replaced by a cold, driving desire to survive.

At once, he releases me, pitching me forward

through the doors to the inner bedchamber. Lifting the abandoned glass of scotch from the table, he approaches. I glance around for a weapon, anything at all. I will kill him, if I have to. I will kill him and run away into hiding if that's what it takes.

"I admit, I was hoping it would be Elizavetta, she was always so... eager to please. But you are my wife, even if you are a whore, and so I see that it must be you." He's toying with me now, taking a step forward as I step back. He throws his knife aside and when I lunge for it, he grabs me easily with one arm. I thrash against him, but he pulls me into his chest once more then pushes me to the wall, pinning me between his body and it. I scream out, and he takes the opportunity to pour the bittersweet liquor down my throat.

My eyes water instantly and he throws the glass, shattering it across the wall opposite us. With both hands free, he lifts me and carries me, kicking and screaming, to the bed. Crawling on top of me, he covers my mouth, so I bite down. His blood pools into my mouth, gagging me with the thick, metallic taste of it. He pulls his hand away, and then punches me in the face hard enough that I feel bones fracture under the skin.

"You are my wife and you will submit to me, is that clear?" he screams into my face.

I spit his own blood back at him and he rears up onto his knees, hitting me again, only this time in the chest, hard enough to force the air from my lungs and leave me gasping. Rolling off me, he trudges to the doors of the bedchamber and slams them closed, propping a chair under the knobs.

"Now, where were we?" he asks, stripping off his clothes.

By the time he crawls back onto me, the tincture I've laced the brandy with is in full effect. The room grows fuzzy, and my arms and legs become heavy. Everything goes dark and the last thing I remember is the weight of his body on mine before I slip from consciousness.

When I wake, I'm immediately aware of two things, the first is that I'm entirely nude and the second is that every small measure of me has been abused. The pain is everywhere, a throbbing ache covering my entire body. Looking down, I see that I'm covered in newly forming bruises and welts, and large handprints decorate my hips, thighs, and breasts. My head is too heavy to lift fully from the bed, but I manage to cover myself with a blanket. The bed is empty, and Peter is nowhere to be found. I scream, and pain explodes on the side of my face. My throat is dry and rough and I have to scream several times before the sound is loud enough that anyone might hear me.

Maria rushes in, grabbing my robe and carefully pulling back the covers for me. She calls for another of my ladies, who gasps and quickly crosses herself before helping Maria lift me from the bed.

"I've run you a bath with lavender and salts. It should help," she says gently. "With the *other* pains as well."

"How did you know?" I ask.

The maids exchange a look.

"You screamed quite a lot," Maria answers finally.

Every movement is agony as they half-carry me to the tub and help me in. I soak there until the water is like ice, and then have them fill it once more. After I've soaked most of the day away, I sit by the fireplace in my robe, not bothering to dress. There's no way I could put on a corset anyway, just the soft cotton of the robe is aggravating my sensitive skin. Leaving the room isn't even an option.

Peter returns that night. Seeing me sitting by the fire, he orders me to stand. I obey as best I can. When I falter, he takes my hand.

"I'm sorry if I hurt you badly," he says with a sadistic smile.

"No, you aren't," I say flatly, too hurt and tired to even pretend to humor him.

He raises his eyebrows and kisses my hand gently. "You're right, I'm not."

I flinch. The wine and whiskey I've been indulging in are taking the edge off the pain, but the ache is still there.

"Take off your robe," he orders.

I glare at him.

"You can take it off or I can cut it off," he says pleasantly. "Personally, I find I like it when you make it a challenge."

I step around him slowly, reaching for the bottle of brandy and taking a long, deep drink of it before setting it back down. Turning to him, I untie the robe and let it slip to the floor. He rushes at me, like a starving man might rush to a banquet table, and captures my mouth with his. I bite at his lips and he pulls away, grinning. Lifting me, he carries me off. The brandy acts much faster this time, and I'm unconscious before we even hit the bed.

Chapter
NINETEEN

The days go on in this manner for some time. Eventually, he takes the laced brandy away, saying he prefers it when I fight back, but I stop giving him the satisfaction. Eventually, the worst of my injuries heal and I'm able to function somewhat normally again. Peter, however, has other ideas. He's forbidden me to leave my room or see anyone other than my maids. I've gone from being a ruler to being a prisoner in my own palace. Sergei comes every day, seeking an audience, and every day, I send him away. The shame and guilt is crippling as I lie in bed, refusing to even eat. The odor of the food is noxious to me, and weak as I am, it is my spirit that is most injured. I cannot stop Peter from taking me as he wants. He is my husband and it is his right by law. This is not some grand fairy tale. No one is coming to rescue me from my ivory tower. Despair consumes me until finally, overwhelmed with concern, Maria sends for the physician.

He's disturbed, that much I can ascertain from

his expression. My arms and legs are bruised, though healing, and my face is no longer swollen or sore.

"When was your last course?" he asks, counting the pulse in my wrist.

My head lulls to the side as I try to remember. "The final week of August, I believe."

He drops my wrist and pats my hand gently. "Well, that's likely the problem then. You're with child."

I roll over and look at him. He's pleased, but I can't muster up anything but loathing. "What day is it?" I ask. Surely not so much time has passed.

"It's October the twelfth," he says slowly. "I will report your condition to the grand duke. After your last loss, we should move you to your own private rooms and begin your confinement early."

I can see in his expression his true motive. He's concerned that the abuse will continue despite my condition, and he wants me moved away from Peter for my own protection. If I weren't so tired, I would embrace him.

"The grand duke is lucky to have you," he says gently. "The lords will be pleased to know your long absence from court was due to such happy circumstances. They will be most relieved to see you again."

His words are calm and carefully chosen, but their meaning is clear. Peter is upsetting the lords again and they, probably fearing for my life, have been worried. A thought occurs to me, something I'd failed to realize before. If the lords thought Peter had hurt me—possibly killed me even—they would stand against him with the empress. They would support her passing him over for the crown, either to my child or another candidate.

"I will tell Peter the news," I decide, rallying my strength enough to sit up. "Please relate my thanks to the lords for their well wishes and tell them that I will be returning to court soon."

Peter has been back less than a month and I know well that odds are the child isn't even his, not that he will ever hear those words from me. Finally, I have within my grasp something that has been absent from me for far too long. Once more, I have leverage against my husband. I feel my strength returning as, for the first time in weeks, my hope returns.

I call my maids and begin the slow process of restoring myself to life, all the while plotting how best to use this to my advantage. He won't touch me now; he wouldn't risk the child. In that much, at least, I am protected. The empress will be pleased with me once more, and in her good graces, I could always ask to return to Winter Palace for my confinement, should Peter become too intolerable.

I've bathed, dressed, and I'm in the process of having my things moved when Peter stomps into the room.

"And where are you running off to?" he demands.

"The physician came to see me today. I'm with

child once more."

I'm not sure what reaction I expect, he'd been so overjoyed the last time I handed him such news, but he's grown colder now, and simple as he is, even he must suspect the child might not be his. His expression crumbles immediately, a look of fear riding across his furrowed brow.

"I thought you would be pleased. This was your ultimate goal, wasn't it? The reason you've been forcing yourself upon me with such vigor?" I ask. He doesn't answer so I turn my back to him, removing my tiara from its box. "Either way, the deed is done now. And I am moving to private chambers on advice of the physician."

I turn to him and he's staring up at me, dumbfounded. "Whose side are you on? Will you agree to the empress' plot to pass me over and make your child her heir?" he asks.

I frown. Would I support such a thing? There is a hatred, a bitterness in my heart that says yes, I would. But then I would never rule, never be empress. Most likely, she would send Peter and me away and take the child from us as she once took young Peter from his family. No, I would not support that. Being mother of the heir would give me stability, but being wife to the Emperor would give me power. And I've fought too hard and sacrificed too much to relent now.

"No," I answer. "I would not allow her to pass you over, even in favor of our child. And if you will allow me to continue what I began here, to sway the lords to your side, we will gather enough support that she will dare not even try."

He nods. "There is an ally in Moscow; he is a favorite of hers but a friend to me. He is the only one who voiced opposition to her plot. I will travel there to seek his council. You will accompany me."

I nod. "But know this, you will not touch me again. If you ever lay a hand upon me again, I *will* kill you. Do you understand?"

I expect anger or retribution, but he just blinks up at me like a schoolboy who has been chastised. "Yes."

I run my hands down my skirts. "Good. We will leave for Moscow in three days. Have everything prepared. My ladies and I will take the carriage. You will ride with the guards."

"Three days ago, you wouldn't even rise from bed, now you order me about like a servant," he muses. "What has spun you about so quickly?"

I straighten, lowering my chin and holding his eye determinedly while I slip my tiara onto my head. "I've been reminded that the only ally you truly have is me. You can't hurt me anymore. You need me, not just for the child, but also to stand with you against the empress. I will bring the nobles to kneel at your feet, and I will supply the love of the people that you will require to rule. You need me, and I know it. Your power over me is truly gone."

"I could wait until the child is born and have you

killed," he mutters petulantly.

"Hollow threats, Peter. Even with an heir, all that prevents the empress from passing you over is the support of the lords, and to keep their support, you need me."

It's hard not to sound smug, but when I look at him now, he seems so small and frail. His face is badly scarred and his golden-yellow hair is thinning. My once-beautiful husband is withering before me. I shouldn't be glad of it, but I am. Even as he grows weak, I grow strong.

"If you will excuse me, I am going to go discuss some urgent matters with Sergei." I expect a word of rebuke, a harsh reprimand for my boldness, but Peter just nods as I take my leave.

Once I'm out the door, I press my hand gently to my belly, silently praying to all the hosts of heaven that the child is, indeed, Sergei's.

If no one is going to save me, I'd best get on with saving myself.

Sergei is so glad to see me that it takes the better part of an hour before I can pry myself free of his desperate embrace.

"I was so worried, so afraid that he'd hurt you, or worse." His face is flush, his dark hair ragged as he kisses me again, stealing my breath. When I finally pull away, he traces the fading bruises on my arms, neck, and the side of my face. "I think I went mad. I would have killed him with my bare hands to get to you. It was only Maria's merciful words that gave me peace. She told me you were alive, but ill and refusing to see anyone. Please, please for my sanity, never do that again, never refuse me so."

I smile against his fingertips as they cross my lips. "I promise."

He leans in for more kisses, but I hold him off with a hand to his chest. "I have news first. I'm with child again," I say pleasantly.

Swooping me up in his arms, he carries me off to the settee in my office and proceeds to demonstrate his joy.

After, as I lay there in his arms, I have to make my confession. "Peter did hurt me. I've never been so terrified or felt so powerless in my entire life. For a time, I wanted to die. It was only the thought of returning to you that kept me from faltering, I want you to know that." I take a deep breath, and his arms tighten around me. "And I want you to know that I will never feel that powerless ever again, whatever it takes. I swear to God I will burn this palace to the ground before I let Peter or Elizabeth hold such power over me again."

"It kills me that I could not protect you from him," Sergei whispers gently. "But I swear to you, I will never let him hurt you again."

"The best way you can help me now is to help me to convince the empress not to pass over Peter. Without a crown on my head, I cannot hope to survive this place. It is a fragile game, and I've come to realize that in order to win, I must be the player holding all the cards."

"What would you have me do?" he asks.

I pause, unsure of the task I'm about to request of him. The rational part of my mind knows what I need him to do, but the other part of me wants nothing more than to hold him close and never release him from my side.

"I need you to go to the Winter Palace and speak to her. Convince her that Peter is sound in mind and body. Tell her that with me at his side, we can control the court and rule the nation successfully, with the support of the nobles. I fear the influence of others in this matter. She will listen to you."

"You are sending me off to defend the man who hurt you, the man whom I was recently planning to kill myself?" He laughs dryly. "And what if she will not listen?"

"Make her listen," I say flatly.

He raises one dark eyebrow, "What are you asking me to do? Are you suggesting I should rekindle my relationship with her to hold her ear?"

I sit up quickly. "Absolutely not."

He laughs, and this time, it's deep and warm. "I know, I was only teasing. I like it when you get jealous."

I grin and nibble on my lower lip, resigning to get up and straighten myself. After a few minutes, and with his help, I'm presentable once more.

"Peter and I are traveling to Moscow. He says he has an ally there, but I suspect it might be a ploy." He frowns, his expression growing worried. "I'll take Grigori with me, don't fret. But I should be there. There will be ample chance to meet the villagers along the way and to speak with a few of the nobles who still remain tied to the Imperial Court. I must win them to our side as well."

He seizes me by the chin. "Win them to your side. Let Peter be the bungling ruffian he is, but win their loyalty to you. The wind is changing—I've been around long enough to witness it before—and you never know what direction it will blow next. Just be careful, and keep our child safe for me. Promise me."

"I promise," I say, earning me one last kiss.

Chapter
TWENTY

The ride to Moscow is long and bitter cold. We are forced to stop and rest in tents overnight. They don't provide much protection from the bitter cold. Each morning, we wake to a thin layer of frost on the sturdy canvas. I spend most nights sharing a bed with Maria, more for warmth than companionship. Sergei is far away in St. Petersburg as I asked, and I try to keep my mind occupied to keep from the aching loss of him.

It takes over a week to reach the Estate of Count Chernyshev, Peter's ally. Also in residence are the Countess Shuvalova, one of the empress' ladies, and Kyril Razumovsky, one of the lords on her privy council. It feels to me less like being welcomed into a home as it does walking into a cage full of lions.

They welcome us with a grand banquet and night after night of operas and military drills, all the while expressly avoiding Peter's every attempt to raise the matter for which we'd come. Two weeks into our visit, another of the empress' council arrives, Lord

Baturin. He's young, younger perhaps than even Peter, and light of foot. He dances away in his light blue and green costume, all the while reminding me of a preening peacock.

"This is the man we've been waiting for," Peter mumbles over the rim of his glass. "He's been at her side for weeks, gauging her reaction at the news of your pregnancy."

I glare at the man, trying to size him up. I realize two things immediately. Firstly, he smiles too much and too falsely. Every conversation is amusement to him as he flatters and gestures flamboyantly. A dandy, my mother would call him. But there's something else, something that strikes me secondly. The smile is a careful façade. I watch as his eyes dart back and forth. Even in his merriment, he is silently taking stock of everyone in the room to the tiniest detail. The telltale mark of a skilled spy, playing the fool and keeping those around him at ease, while he plots silently. He is, more than any of the others, dangerous and will need to be handled carefully.

I open my mouth to share my observations with Peter but stop short when Baturin slides over to our table.

He bows deeply. "Your Graces, might I have the honor of a dance with the grand duchess?"

Peter smiles and lists his glass. He's already drank more than he should and I'm afraid to leave his side, afraid he will say more than he should. "Of course, be my guest."

I have no choice now; to refuse would be the height of rudeness. Taking his arm, I allow him to lead me to the dance floor where we join the other dancers, taking our places. The music begins and we weave back and forth, carefully performing our steps. When we draw close, he engages me in conversation.

"I'm glad to see you well, Your Grace. Though I'm surprised that you dared to make the trek in your condition."

I smile. "Not at all, the fresh air is good for me. Besides, we thought it would be good to travel a bit, get to know every piece of our country before we are called upon to rule it."

He raises an eyebrow. "Is that so? I've heard the grand duke only cares for his small duchy of Holstein. That is it all he cares to hear about."

"Well, perhaps he does inquire about it often. It was his birthplace and thus has some sentimental value to him, but he is eager to get to know the other lands as well," I answer coolly.

It doesn't bother me too much to admit that he's right about Peter's limited interest in the country. What does bother me is how he is so keenly aware of it. "What of you, Lord Baturin? Where do you call home?"

He smiles one of his phony smiles, and it's all I have not to cringe at the sight of it. "St. Petersburg is my home now, though I was born and raised in the north. My family rules a large fishing village."

"How lovely," I say absently.

"Fond of fishing, are you?"

I smile pleasantly. "I find there is nothing so marvelous as the sea air to calm a person."

He nods in agreement.

We continue to banter as we dance. I keep getting the feeling he's trying to lead me somewhere in the conversation, attempting to coerce me to speaking out of turn, but I do not falter.

"And what do you think of the empress?" he asks, doing away with his pretense altogether.

"I think she is as shrewd as she is beautiful. She is a grand ruler for Russia and a great example to Peter and me," I say flatly.

With that, the music ends. I return to my seat beside Peter, who slaps the table excitedly at something that's been said and stands, laughing with the count. He leans over to me.

"We are going to go enjoy some brandy. I will see you in your chambers later," he slurs.

I raise one eyebrow in silent challenge. We haven't shared a bed since I discovered my condition and if he thinks he is going to stumble drunkenly into it tonight...

He winks mischievously and takes his leave, abandoning me to the merriment of the countess. A dour woman in her late forties, the Countess Chernyshev is a large, uncouth woman. She always has her mouth full and often belches loudly. I learn she was a peasant, as she tells me the story of how she came to meet the count, when he was a young noble. She spins a tale of torrid romance under the nose of their parents.

"The wedding was done in secret, of course, before I opened my legs to him. He would have done anything I asked for one good roll in the hay." She laughs loudly, being quite taken with drink herself. "But when his family found out, well, there was a bit of hell to pay. That's why he gets to run off to Court and I have to stay here you see. It was quite a scandal. No doubt they still gossip about it."

I nod, though if they do, it's never reached my ears. Court can be fickle like that; today's scandal is tomorrow's forgotten history. Of course, had he not married her, she would have been utterly ruined. For him, it would have been a minor indiscretion only. That is the politics of womanhood, of nobility over peasantry.

She talks until I'm far too bored to care. At some point, Lord Baturin heads off to join Peter and the Count and I excuse myself to my chamber. Maria stays behind, with my blessing, to chat with Lord Razumovsky, a dashing man in his early thirties. He's wealthy, handsome, and by everything I've witnessed in the past days, a kind and loyal gentleman. He is in need of a wife, and she would be a good fit, if the interest were mutual. From the way she is looking at him when I leave, it is.

Grigori, my constant shadow, follows me to my room and takes up watch outside my door. He's distant and cool, not nearly as informal as he once had been. I think he feels similar to Sergei, that he failed to protect me, to honor his oath to me. But there was nothing he could have done, and I've told him as much. It doesn't seem to change anything.

Once alone in my room, I open a book and settle in to read for a while. I assume by Peter's gesture that he wants to speak with me privately after his meeting, and I doubt I can manage myself out of my gown before Maria arrives to help me anyway. I could call a maid, I suppose, but I decide to wait it out with my book of philosophies.

Sometime later, when Peter arrives, I've fallen asleep in my chair, my book still open on my lap. His boisterous entrance wakes me and I tense.

He holds a hand out. "Don't worry. I've not come to ravish you."

I frown but say nothing. He laughs and half falls into the chair across from me. "I finally spoke to them about the empress' threat." He pauses, belching loudly. "And they have told me that just this week, Elizabeth retracted the statement. Even with news of your pregnancy, she has agreed to preserve the line of succession as it stands now."

I feel myself sag with relief, the weariness of the trip finally soaking into my bones.

"Apparently, your Sergei was quite instrumental in changing her mind," he says, as if hinting at some sort of impropriety. I let the remark go, unwilling to give voice to my own thoughts on the matter.

"I'm very glad." I say flatly.

"There is more. They have come up with a clever plot to see me safely to the throne." He is on the edge of his seat now, eager as a little boy.

"What plot?" I ask, perking up.

"Baturin wants to kill the empress, set fire to Winter Palace so it looks as if she died in an accident, then put me on the throne immediately," he says, his voice high with excitement. "Just think, we could have her out of our way permanently. You and I could take our places as rulers. We could make Oranienbaum the new center of power in Russia."

My mouth has gone dry as I try to breathe slowly and process his words. "Do you realize what you're saying?" I ask, barely able to push the words through my scratchy throat. "Not only is it treason just to speak those words, but it would be regicide to even know about such a thing, much less endorse it. Her blood would be on your hands."

He throws his hands in the air. "It's not wrong if it's God's will. How can I sit here and abide while that treacherous whore sits on my throne? She is evil to her very core. She's already turned against Prussia, abandoning the nation that supported her, but she's swayed by whatever handsome face is currently in her bed."

"This isn't about her rule," I chastise. "She's hurt your feelings, wounded your pride. I understand that, I feel the sting of it as well. If you knew the things she said to me when you took ill, the things she wanted me to do... But even so, we cannot be party to this plot. Surely, you understand that?"

"Bah. What do you know? You're no better than her," he says, turning away from me. The sting of his words is sharp and brutal.

"Do you really think so little of me?" I ask, a soft whisper.

When his gaze swings back to mine, I know he meant his cruel words, and I wonder, if only for a moment, if he's right.

"We will leave this place immediately," I say, pacing the floor. "Send word that rumors of a plot against her reached our ears and that we left as soon as we heard them. Tell her, our loyalty, as always, is with her."

Now, he's enraged. "Why would I do such a thing? These men love me; they want to see me on the throne."

"Or," I offer, "it's a trap. Think about it, most of these men are at the very heart of her council. If she truly wanted to pass you over for the throne, what better way than to condemn you for being part of a plot against her? She could hang you for treason if it struck her fancy, or at best, have you exiled."

His mouth slams closed with an audible click of

teeth.

"Peter, I beg you. Leave this place and report this plot. Let her see that you are loyal, or at least shrewd enough not to be manipulated by idle promises. Let her think you are on her side. Give her no reason to judge you unworthy of the throne." My words escape in a desperate rush.

He shakes his head, looking as though he desperately wants to argue, but can't find fault with my reasoning. Finally, after a crushingly long silence, he speaks. "We will leave tomorrow. But I will not offer them a word of support in it, nor will I say anything of this to the empress. If their plan succeeds, then well done. If not, we pretend it never reached our ears."

I know that not reporting it is a miscalculation. If the plan fails and one or more of the men are questioned, they will surely tell her of Peter's foreknowledge, if not making up stories of his involvement just to avoid the rack. No, as soon as we leave this place, I will send my own messenger to Elizabeth, with word of all that has transpired here. If it is a plot on her part, to trap Peter, then no harm will come to anyone. If, however, it is a genuine bid to remove her from the throne, then we will either once more be in her good graces for reporting it, or we will be the innocent recipients of a revolt we had no part of.

Either way, our hands will be clean of this mess.

Peter finally drifts off in his drunken stupor, and I call the valet and the stewards to carry him to his own room. Just the gin-soaked smell of him in my chamber is enough to turn my stomach. I remain quite determined that he will never sleep in the same room as me ever again.

Maria greets me that morning with news of a proposal.

"Don't you think it's a bit rushed?" I ask, secretly envying her the rush of blood in her cheeks that only comes with infatuation. I've never seen her complexion so rosy or her smile so wide.

"He's just wonderful. I know we've only known each other a few weeks, but I can't imagine anyone making me happier."

I smile, standing and retrieving a small, blue box from my drawer. "Then I am happy for you, and give my blessing warmly. Here, a token of my joy."

She takes the box and opens it to find a pair of stunning gold and pearl ear baubles inside. "They are lovely, thank you, Your Grace."

"Please, call me Catherine," I say, tossing aside propriety long enough to embrace the woman who has grown to be my friend.

How I will miss her.

Preparations for the long journey home begin immediately. Peter tells them I'm feeling unwell and that we must return to Oranienbaum before my condition becomes too precarious for travel. It's not far from the truth. My stomach is always uneasy now, and most of the food here is too heavily salted for my tastes, making it difficult to eat anything, much less to keep it from coming back up again. My hands and feet have begun to swell and my back aches constantly.

As soon as I'm able to, I write a letter to the empress and give it to Grigori, who passes it to his most-trusted lieutenant to take directly to the Winter Palace.

The journey home is taxing, though this time we travel slower, stopping to spend evenings with various nobles on the way through the countryside. It's important for Peter to know them, and for them to know us. It also gives me the opportunity to offer gifts and favors to our hosts, ingratiating them to us. I do my best to charm the lords and befriend the ladies. I make pleasant conversation with so many people of rank and station I can scarcely remember their names. Each evening, I make notes about the people we've met, their needs and their desires. I make careful note of not just their demeanor, but of any secrets or gossip Maria can wrangle from the household. Other than the fairly commonplace lechery and adultery, only a few times am I shocked by these accusations. But I say nothing, just continuing to make friends and to make notes. Peter hunts, charms, and dazzles as if the pox never happened. Only in his semi-regular nightly visits to discuss the day's meetings does his mind occasionally blunder, a forgotten name here, an unfortunate slip of the tongue there. It's enough to make me wonder if his face wasn't the only thing damaged by the disease.

The journey home takes over three weeks.

We are greeted by the nobles in residence when we return. Plans for Maria's wedding are well underway, and despite my exhaustion, I'm genuinely excited for her. Rina greets me with her tiny bundle in her arms. I never imagined a time would come when such a sight didn't cut me to my marrow, but I feel nothing but joy as I kiss the top of his tiny head. Even Peter is in a fine mood as he greets Alexander with a hug and a slap on the back. We catch eyes, but only for a moment, and I am beyond relieved when there is no spark, no remaining embers of emotion smoldering there. Just a subtle peace between us.

All seems well in our little corner of the world, but deep inside me, there is a feeling, a clock ticking, counting down until the time will come and all this happiness is once more burnt to ash in my mouth.

When I catch sight of Sergei waiting in the drawing room, he smiles at me and it's all I have not to pick up my skirts and run to him like a child. Then I see what's in his hands, a neatly folded letter, from the empress no doubt. When I approach, I quickly dismiss my ladies and he bows deeply.

"How was Winter Palace?" I ask.

He tilts his head. "Much the same. The empress

is in fits over King Fredrick's invasion of Austria, and she's worried he will advance on the western border. She sends troops to aid Queen Maria Theresa, but refuses requests for ammunition and supplies."

I shrug. "The war will be over soon. We can only bicker for so long before we remember that we are more powerful together than apart."

"You seem well," he says, offering me his arm as we walk.

"I am, mostly. Tired and feeling quite bulbous at the moment, but all is well. Mother wrote to me to tell me she and my family have gone to Paris to weather the storm of war there. I think she's trying to arrange my sister's marriage to a nephew of the Dauphin."

"Isn't your sister barely seven?" he asks, his tone amused more than horrified.

"Twelve now, but I doubt Mother's efforts will bear any fruit."

"Best not underestimate her. She did manage to wed you to Peter," he adds.

It's difficult not to scoff at the idea that my mother was responsible for my current station. "She may have facilitated my station here, but it was I who won over the empress. Let's not forget that Elizabeth loathed my mother so much I had to send her away lest she bungle the whole affair."

He nods. "A fair point. Speaking of the empress, she sends her love as well as a token of her gratitude. A chest of kopecks has been delivered to your chamber."

Good, I think wryly. Let her pay to soothe her guilty heart. I have places enough to use such money.

"And," he continues. "She also sends this."

He holds out the letter, and I tear into it without waiting to arrive at my chamber. I feel myself frown, and then relax as I exhale deeply.

"It says Baturin was taken prisoner directly after we left. Count Chernyshev turned him in for plotting treason. She says that under interrogation, he revealed that he'd spoken to Peter about it, but that Peter did not offer support in the matter. She says, *I would not have believed my nephew capable of such loyalty and forethought if not for your letter condemning the whole affair*. Good. The rift between them seems healed, for now."

"At least until the next time Peter is slighted and decides to do something rash."

My eyes flicker up to him, and he grins. "How do you manage to handle so well all these terribly difficult men in your life?"

I return his smile. "You speak as if I have an army of men like puppets under my control. Do you accuse me of witchcraft?"

Pulling me into my chamber and closing the door behind him, he pulls me into his arms. "Is that your secret? Because you have thoroughly enchanted me, my little queen."

I kiss him, and it's as if everything else falls away. Relaxing against his strong chest, I let myself dissolve into the moment.

Chapter
TWENTY-ONE

The winter passes slowly, each day achingly long and dull. It's a relief when spring finally arrives and I begin my confinement. No more lavish balls or dreary meetings with the privy council, I'm freed to spend my days lost in books, and I devour them in earnest, one after another. Maria visits and we talk about her wedding, which unfortunately I'm going to miss, thanks to my condition. Sergei sneaks in whenever he can, filling me in on all the court goings-on. Mostly, I just like to lay my head on his chest and listen to the sound of his voice. Even Rina comes by, bringing her quickly growing child. He looks more like his father with each passing day, and I find myself surprised by the impatience I feel to hold my own child in my arms. We play cards and chess and talk about the latest gossip.

Soon, I begin to feel him, moving about in my belly. It's an alien sensation, but not at all unpleasant. I talk to him and read to him. It's as if I exist in my own little bubble world, a calm, if solitary, existence, and a much-needed respite.

Spring comes and goes in the blink of an eye. I watch Maria's wedding from my window and when she comes to say goodbye, my heart breaks a little. I reinstate Rina as my Maid of Honor, since they seem to have no plans to leave the palace. She tells me Alexander is glad to be at Peter's side once more, though she also tells me Peter's wild ways have returned. He's still drinking heavily and taking several young women to his bed, none of whom stay for very long. I'm too content to be concerned, however.

One day in early June, I've finally grown so round I can barely toddle around my chamber, so I send my maids to fetch me some books from the library. They return with a huge stack, and I begin rummaging through them. A familiar volume catches my eye.

John Wilmot's Letters To His Mistress.

Perhaps it's the emotional nature of pregnancy or the fact that I haven't seen Sergei in several days, but I feel a tear escape my eye as I run my fingers along the spine.

It's not the same copy that once held the illicit letters to my would-be lover, but it's enough to make me sentimental for the innocent, naïve girl I'd been. It seems like a lifetime ago. My eyes flick up to Rina, who is reading a book of her own in the seat across the room. Her face is serene, and for the briefest of moments, an old jealousy flairs. It's gone as quickly as it had come, but I'm left feeling guilty. She'd been forced to marry Alexander, and that was my fault. How could I be upset that she'd grown to love him as I had, and that he'd grown to love her in return? I genuinely love them both, so when these fleeting moments of sadness arise, I know there is something wrong.

At that moment, a ripple of pain washes over me, clenching tight like a belt around my stomach. I cry out, dropping the book to the floor. "Rina, fetch the midwife," I order, standing up on wobbly legs and making my way to the labor bed that's been prepared for me.

❧

The pain comes in waves, ebbing and cresting in nauseating frequency. Peter is gone hunting with Alexander and Mikhail, so that leaves Sergei as the only nervous man outside my door. I don't want to frighten him, so I try to stay as quiet as possible until the pain intensifies so suddenly I cry out.

The baby comes after just a few hours, at least they tell me it's only been a few hours, for to me, it feels like days. An easy birth, the midwife says, making me want to reach out and slap her soundly.

Still, I don't faint and when they place the tiny bundle in my arms, I nearly cry out with joy. His tiny eyes are blue, but with a slight hint of green that betrays his true father. I carefully count each finger and toe, memorizing each fascinating detail.

I know I can't send for Sergei, I can't present his son into his arms, and the grief of it hits me full force only when I hear him weeping from behind the door.

My strong, proud, brave Sergei. Father to a child that will never be his.

"Shall I wash him?" Rina asks gently.

I want to refuse, the desire to keep him in my arms forever is nearly impossible to deny.

"Perhaps Lord Salkov will assist me," she says, her voice a whisper.

I nod, handing the soft, small bundle into her arms.

While the nurses and maids tend to me, an envoy is sent to the Winter Palace to deliver the news to the empress. I expect she will want to come and inspect the baby for herself, so I tell the maids to make the necessary preparations. I know that I will only have a few short weeks of respite, alone with my baby, before I will have to rejoin court, and I intend to enjoy every moment of it. Once I'm cleaned and dressed, they bring the bassinet into my chamber, at my request.

"Surely you want the babe to sleep with the wet nurse," the midwife says.

I snap at her. "He is my child, and I will feed him."

My ladies look aghast. It's not protocol, I know that, but I hadn't known just how desperately I would love the little creature from the moment I set eyes on him. Motherhood will be my bliss, I decide, carefully folding the tiny blankets on the table before finally taking to my own bed and falling into an exhausted sleep.

I wake to the sound of the baby crying. The nurse is rocking him gently, but I sit up and motion for her to deliver him to me.

"How do I feed him?" I ask even as he turns, nuzzling into my chest.

She shows me, and soon he is eating well. He's strong for such a tiny creature, and has a fuzz of dark brown hair like mine on a spot on the very back of his head. Soon, he's full and content and despite the nurse's objections, I continue to hold him close as he sleeps.

The door to my chamber flies open with no preamble, startling us all. The empress strides in. Donning a full, red riding habit, she strips off her gloves excitedly. Peter is close at her heels.

"I rode out as soon as your message arrived," she says curtly, motioning the nurse to take the baby.

In walk three priests of Her Majesty's Synod, the church's representatives in matters of state. Their robes are blood red, their faces grim even in the face of the young prince. Behind the empress, Peter puckers his mouth in silent revolt. He's never converted to the Orthodox Church, and I know it burns him to have the baby blessed and baptized into the faith.

The holy men take turns blessing the child, the last anointing him with holy oil and saying, "Young

Prince of Russia, it is by the will of God and by Imperial decree that we give you the name, Paul Petrovitch. May you be blessed by his glory all your days."

They funnel out of the room quickly, and I'm at a loss to explain the rushed nature of the naming. Normally, the formal naming is done in the Great Hall, a lavish and very public affair. Something about the secrecy of it unsettles me deeply, but I know I cannot give voice to my fears and doubts, not at this moment.

Turning back to me, Elizabeth hands me a tray laden with what must be hundreds of thousands of rubles, a gold box filled with jewels, and three large diamond rings.

"You have done your part admirably," she says coldly. "We will have the baptism at Winter Palace in six days. Peter will attend."

"Will I not be allowed?" I ask, a dry lump forming in my throat. I'm beginning to form a clear picture of her motivation. A formal naming would have required my presence, but now she could move forward without me. She is cutting me from his life already. I feel a tear slip down my cheek as a hollowness opens like a chasm in my soul.

"No. You should remain in confinement for another forty days before returning to court. It is for your own safety, to make sure you've properly healed."

I weakly thank her for her gift and her concern, though the extended confinement feels more like a prison sentence than a kindness, and she nods absently, her attention fixed on Paul's small face as he begins to fuss. I hold my arms out to take my child, but the empress snaps her fingers and motions for the nurse to follow her from the room. They exit in a rush of skirts, taking my baby with them. Peter lags behind. I mean to ask him why they've taken Paul and when he will be returned to me, but his expression betrays the truth I'd only begun to realize.

The empress has taken my child—permanently.

The shaking begins immediately, as my arms, once warm from holding his small body, grow cold. I cry out as the pain engulfs me, a deep emptiness like nothing I've ever known filling my heart. He turns from me and leaves without a word, abandoning me to my misery. I cry through the night and well into the next day, until there's nothing left but the void inside me. Finally, when night comes again, Sergei steals into my room. I'm unable to find joy at seeing him, and not even the feel of his arms cradling me eases the suffering.

"She took him," I mutter over and over.

He strokes my hair, soothing me as best he is able. "I know, darling, I know."

When I'm finally calm again, Sergei tips my chin up and brushes a kiss over my lips.

"There is other news as well," he begins. I know from his tone it is not of a glad nature. "The empress has ordered me to take word of the birth to Sweden. I'm to leave tomorrow."

"Sweden? You will be away from me for months. How will I survive alone, especially now?" It's as if she's ripped out my heart. I can feel it breaking in my chest, and the pain is enough to make me retch. "She is taking everyone I love away from me."

He nods sadly. "I will be back before your confinement ends. I know it pains you to have the babe taken so soon, but there is no denying her in this."

"She is trying to break me," I say quietly, more to myself than to him. "Her cruelty knows no bounds."

"Yes, I suspect she is trying to break you," he agrees. "But you will not break. You are stronger than she is."

I shake my head. "I don't feel strong."

"I know, but you have one thing she doesn't. You have the capacity to not only love, but to love deeply and with your entire being. It's that love that makes you feel weak, but it is exactly that love that makes you powerful. Think about it, is there anything you would not do, any length you would not go to, to protect the people you love?"

I don't have to think about it, the answer is obvious. "No."

"Then use this pain, turn it to your advantage. Make it your strength."

He's right. As soon as he says it, I feel the pain begin to twist inside me, bending into a new form, a cold, steely resolve.

From there, my course becomes very clear. I can

trace all my suffering back not to Peter or my mother, but to the empress herself. And it is time she paid for my misery.

Chapter
TWENTY-TWO

I watch from my window as the fireworks rip across the night sky to celebrate the birth of the heir. Below me, I hear the cannonades and balls raging well into the night for nearly seventeen straight days. All the while, I am reading, studying, and more importantly, I am planning my next moves carefully.

I don't see my son again until November first, when the Nobles of Court and the foreign ambassadors come to my chamber to extend a formal congratulation. Many of them leave gifts and tokens, all of which are quickly scooped up by Peter. "For the royal treasury." The empress stands across the room, my babe in her arms. The sound of his cries only adds fire to my determination. I watch her with stern eyes even as I'm greeted warmly by the assembly. They fuss and fawn over me in ways that, judging by her sour expression, the empress greatly disapproves of. Any other time I may have sent them away, feigning exhaustion, but I don't. I bask in their adoration and watch as the empress grows more and more jealous.

It's petty, to be sure, but I promise myself that I will never, from this moment on, miss an opportunity to cause her grief, as she has so often caused me.

On February tenth, the final day of my confinement, Sergei still has not returned. The empress seems content to force him to continue traveling, sending word of the new heir all the way to Paris. He sends letters, on occasion, but all were always quite formal, lest they should be intercepted.

The next day is Peter's birthday, and the empress has planned a fantastic ball. The empress sends me word that I may attend, but that she requires I wear blue, and cannot have any lace or ornamental ribbons. It's a sign of her vanity, of how terribly threatened she's become. I have a gown made expressly for the occasion.

When I arrive at the ball, in a gown of royal blue so fine it cost half of my monthly allowance in silk alone. White lace trims the edges and cascades down my back from the elaborate, blue velvet and silver embroidered kokoshnik. It's a very traditional Russian gown and headdress with which I send a clear message to the assembly. Many have considered me a German Princess, a foreigner. But in this one bold statement, I clearly say that I am of Russia, even more so then Peter who, as always, is in his Prussian-inspired suit. I am one of them. That is my first message. The second is in open defiance of Elizabeth's letter. She wanted me to make my re-entrance into court as a barely noticed whisper, but as soon as the page announces me and I enter the room, all eyes are on me. The entire assembly dips into low bows and formal curtsies, just as they would for the empress herself. When they are all lowered, I catch a glimpse of Elizabeth from across the room. Her face is flustered, her red and gold gown not nearly as fine as mine, and looking quite bloated and puffy. I smile at her with all the bravado I can muster in the moment before the assembly rises.

It's Alexander who greets me, and escorts me to my seat beside Peter. "You look as lovely as the first time I laid eyes on you," he whispers.

"Thank you," I say, unsure how to respond to his words. His tone seems innocent enough, but perhaps it is as Sergei said, perhaps past loves never truly leave our hearts.

The empress says nothing at my arrival, but whispers to Chancellor Besthuvez, ever her companion. I dine beside Peter, who seems not to notice me at all except to bore me with the details of his latest maneuver.

"I've decided to bring a garrison of troops from Holstein," he says, taking a drink.

I clear my throat. "Are you sure that's wise? Bringing Prussian soldiers here, now? We are in the midst of a war, and the troops already fear you favor the Germans."

He waves me off. "They are my people. I am still the Duke of Holstein, after all. I cannot abandon them just because my aunt can't keep her head with matters of state."

I don't say more. His words are dangerous, but his tone is defiant. Perhaps I can use it to my advantage in the future.

The evening rolls on, and parade after parade of spectacle followed by the largest cake I've ever seen. By the night's end, everyone is very full, very drunk, and very tired.

Everyone, that is, except for me.

The next morning, I'm playing cards with Rina when the empress' steward arrives, with a reprimand. "The empress reminds you that you are not to wear ribbon or lace or ornament of any kind to the balls while she is in residence at Oranienbaum."

I nod. "Please tell Her Majesty that I send my apologies if I offended her. I only assumed her merit was not a matter of beauty, clothes, or ornament, for when the first has faded, the others become ridiculous. Only one's character endures. But if I have displeased her, please beg her forgiveness and ask if she might attend tea with me tomorrow, that I might seek her forgiveness."

He nods and leaves quickly, his face twitching as if restraining a laugh.

"That is a dangerous game to play," Rina cautions me.

"Games are one thing I have grown exceedingly good at, what with all this free time on my hands," I say, laying down my cards.

That night, I wear my simplest white gown. I don't bother to powder or pin my hair, instead leaving it free to fall in dark waves over my bare shoulders, a simple, white ribbon tied around my head. I wear no jewels, no adornment of any kind, not even my tiara. Upon examining myself in the mirror, I imagine I might look a bit like an angel, a vengeful angel carrying down the wrath of God himself, but an angel nonetheless.

The reaction of the assembly is even starker than the previous evening and as before, all attention is on me. I relish it, dancing until my feet are too sore to stand another minute. Even Elizabeth's favorite of the moment, young Alexander Shuvalov, begs my attentions, visibly infuriating her. I flirt and look away, once more playing the delicate game of subtle seduction Madame Groot taught me so long ago. In the eyes of those around me, I see myself clearly, perhaps for the first time. I am a living flame, a phoenix rising from the ashes. And these people, all of them save the empress herself, stand in awe of me.

The next morning, a message comes from the empress. She will join me for tea in the drawing room. Smiling, I open my chest of drawers and remove the small pouch Rina had so carefully procured for me. Dried and powdered horse chestnut seeds.

Chapter

TWENTY-THREE

I arrive early, and the maids prepare the tea. I dismiss them. Once they've gone, I empty most of the liquid into a bottle concealed in my skirts as my hands quake, leaving only enough tea for one person before carefully sprinkling the powder into the kettle. The enormity of my decision is like lead in my bones, a heaviness that I fear I shall carry all my days. Even so, my resolve is set. I have been her victim for far too long already.

The empress arrives soon after with her entourage, all of whom take up seats around us. The maid pours her cup, and then sets about attending the others, only to find she needs more tea and bustles off to the kitchens.

"You wish to seek my forgiveness?" she asks, taking a sip of tea.

"Do I need to? Have I displeased you?" I ask. "I have given you the heir you required. I have even built Peter up so that the nation will accept him as your successor. In what manner have I failed you?" I take a sip of tea and watch as she does the same.

"Your haughtiness displeases me greatly. If you believe your position here to be secure simply because you are mother of the prince, you are greatly mistaken."

"You could send me home," I offer hopefully. It's a risk, asking for such a thing. I must rely on her desire to do anything contrary to what she thinks might bring me joy.

"What about your son?"

I swallow, knowing this lie will taste the most bitter on my tongue. "He is in your loving custody; I have no fear for him. He will be safe and well cared for."

She scoffs, taking another drink. "Even so. I'm afraid I simply cannot allow you to flee back to Prussia. My enemies search for any sign of weakness or instability. The world looks to us now, and we must present a united front against their scrutiny. If you leave, Peter will seem weak. If the nobles lose faith in him..."

She trails off, her hand shaking, her teacup clanking loudly against her saucer.

"Empress, are you unwell?" I ask.

She shakes her head. Vanity to the last.

"Of course not. I'm in perfect health. I think it's only that I tire of you." She stands, and I watch as she wobbles. I stand as well, and curtsy. "You will not leave Oranienbaum. Do not think of it again. And from now on, if you receive a directive from me, you will follow it to the letter. Is that understood?"

"Yes, Your Highness."

I watch her shakily make her exit, heading for her private chamber.

Later that night, I'm woken by the steward in my outer chamber. I put on my robe and race out. "What is it?" I demand.

"The empress has had a stroke," comes his reply.

Licking my lips, I nod and dismiss him, dressing with a slow deliberateness. Admittedly, I expected her to die, not merely take ill. Part of me is glad she survived, that my soul might be spared that sin, at least. But the darker, twisted part wants to finish what I've begun.

There would be no opportunity for that now. Her room is crowded with people, physicians, maids, the chancellor, and even her clergy are present. The only notable absence is Peter, who was likely too drunk to be woken.

I've never seen the empress look so small and frail. Her mouth hangs open at an odd angle, and a dribble of spittle rolls down her chin. She's muttering, but I can't understand her words. One of the priests leans in and begins relaying her words.

"The empress wishes to keep this matter private. No one outside these walls is to know the extent of her illness. She will return to the Winter Palace immediately to recover privately." He pauses, listening again. "The prince, Paul, will accompany her." More muttering, and then, "Should she fail to recover, the succession is to go forward as planned, with Peter ascending to the throne."

A decidedly unhappy murmur spreads through the small crowd. As everyone begins to file out, I stop the chancellor for a quick word.

"You should call Lord Salkov back as well. He may be of great comfort to her in her time of recovery," I say. The truth is, if he is called back to St. Petersburg, it will be that much easier to return him to his position here, though I dare not say so.

He nods warily. "I will send for him straight away. Is there anything else I can do?"

I'm unused to this compliant nature, but I think I best not take advantage of it just now. "Pray for her. Pray for us all," is my only response.

I look over my shoulder, sparing one last glance at the once-mighty empress. I may not have killed her, but I've hobbled her, at least for the time being. I can't help feeling like it is a dangerous situation.

Don't wound anything you can't kill.

My father's words, spoken to me as a child, come back to me now, and I realize it's only a matter of time before I will have to finish what I've begun. For the people I love and the country I've made my own. For justice and spite and to defend myself from anyone who seeks to do me further harm.

I'm going to have to seize the throne of Russia.

The End: Book 2

~Author's Note~

This book contains scenes that may be sensitive to some readers. I included them not to make light of domestic abuse—and make no mistake, any violence against your person either by friend, stranger, or spouse IS abuse—but to illustrate the harsh realities of the time and situation Catherine found herself in. While it wasn't uncommon in the 1700s, we've come a long way since then. If you or someone you know is in a violent or abusive situation, there is help. I highly recommend seeking help via the local authorities or by contacting The National Domestic Violence Hotline at:

1-800-799-7233

Or

http://www.thehotline.org/

Queen of Tomorrow is the second book in the Stolen Empire series. It is YA/Historical Fiction/ Romance loosely based on the life of young Catherine the Great. It is not meant to be a historically accurate representation, but a fanciful tale of one of the greatest rulers who ever lived. Any mistakes, errors, or inconsistencies are mine alone, and are probably on purpose.

As with book one, Queen of Someday, I have included a great deal of historical fact, only to then meddle with it greatly. Most of the characters in the Stolen Empire series are based on historical figures, but the timeline of Catherine's life has been vastly altered to allow for the flow of the tale to go on, unimpeded by the demands of historical fact. I highly suggest that if you wish to know the real and full story, you pick up her autobiography or read *Catherine the Great* by Robert Massie. The Stolen Empire novels are the tales of the young woman who was Sophie, becoming the ruler who would be Catherine the Great. I have taken extensive liberties with the narrative, so if you are looking for solid facts, I suggest you look elsewhere, because you will find many and wide discrepancies here. I did, at all times, try to remain true to the spirit of the story and to the domineering, compelling figure that was Catherine the Great.

Acknowledgements

The amazing people at Clean Teen Publishing for the constant love and support. You have made writing this series a joy from start to finish, and I couldn't imagine a better home for it, or me.

My family; my wonderful (tolerant, understanding, devilishly handsome) husband, my kiddos, my momma, my stellar and disturbingly normal in-laws, my awesome and disturbingly disturbing blood relatives (looking at you, Lisa, Robin, Dee-dee), and my good friends who are like family. I love you guys!

My minion Army and the CTP Street Team. You guys blow me away with your sheer enthusiasm. Love your guts!

My out-of-this-world assistant, Amanda T. *bows at her feet*

The bloggers, The Cover Contessa, Nerd Girl Official, Smitten over Books, I'm a Reader Not a Writer, One Guy's Guide to Goodreads, and SO MANY MORE. You guys and gals rock my socks with all you do not just for my books, but also for all books. You are my rock stars!

Last, but never least, thank YOU, the readers. Thank you for picking up this book and taking this journey with me.

<3

About the Author

Sherry D. Ficklin is a full time writer from Colorado where she lives with her husband, four kids, two dogs, and a fluctuating number of chickens and house guests. A former military brat, she loves to travel and meet new people. She can often be found browsing her local bookstore with a large white hot chocolate in one hand and a towering stack of books in the other. That is, unless she's on deadline at which time she, like the Loch Ness monster, is only seen in blurry photographs.

CPSIA information can be obtained at www.ICGtesting.com
Printed in the USA
LVOW07s0911130515

438194LV00004B/4/P